THE WORLD IS MINE

**More fresh, fly, and flashy books
from Simon Pulse**

wtf
Peter Lerangis

Raven
Snitch
Street Pharm
Allison van Diepen

The Making of Dr. Truelove
Derrick Barnes

THE COME UP

WRITTEN BY LYAH B. LeFLORE

ILLUSTRATED BY DL WARFIELD

THE WORLD IS MINE

SIMON PULSE | New York London Toronto Sydney

SIMON PULSE

An imprint of Simon & Schuster Children's Publishing Division

1230 Avenue of the Americas, New York, NY 10020

First Simon Pulse paperback edition December 2009

Text copyright © 2009 by Lyah B. LeFlore

Illustrations copyright © 2009 by Darrick "DL" Warfield

All rights reserved, including the right of reproduction
in whole or in part in any form.

SIMON PULSE and colophon are registered trademarks of Simon & Schuster, Inc.

For information about special discounts for bulk purchases, please contact
Simon & Schuster Special Sales at 1-866-506-1949
or business@simonandschuster.com.

The Simon & Schuster Speakers Bureau can bring authors to your live event.
For more information or to book an event contact the Simon & Schuster Speakers
Bureau at 1-866-248-3049 or visit our website at www.simonspeakers.com.

Designed by Mike Rosamilia

The text of this book was set in Zapf Ellipitcal 711 BT.

Manufactured in the United States of America

2 4 6 8 10 9 7 5 3 1

Library of Congress Control Number 2009006900

ISBN: 978-1-4169-7963-0

Acknowledgments

Very special thanks to my agent, Amy Schiffman, for your friendship, professional expertise, and guidance; and for stepping in, rolling up your sleeves, and believing in my vision as an author and creative talent. Let's make movies!

To my partner in crime and illustrator, DL Warfield, you are a brilliant creative force to be reckoned with. Let's make history!

To my editor, Michael del Rosario, thank you for your passion, belief, editorial genius, patience, and push to make this book great. From the moment you saw the treatment and proposal, you connected with the material and our vision.

To Cara Petrus, thank you for your artistic direction and valuable creative input.

Special thanks to my amazing Simon Pulse/Simon & Schuster family for your support: Bethany Buck, Mara Anastas, Jennifer Klonsky, Lucille Rettino, Rob Goodman, and Venessa Williams.

Big thanks and hugs to Lisa Warfield and team Warfield (Kaylee and Dakota): The Warfield compound has been a place of solace and incredible creative energy for this project.

Thanks to the Come Up models: Chase Barnes as Blue, Tyler Huber as Collin, Jeremy Howell as Tommy aka Whiteboy, Bijon Hill as Jade, Christy Anderson (aka Baby Spinderella) as Mamie, and Jordan Lindsay as Trevaughn aka Young Tre. DL and I thank you for rolling the dice with us and believing in the possibilities of The Come Up. Each of you embodies the true spirit of these characters, and I look forward to bringing them to life with you.

And enormous thanks to the parents for "getting it": Spinderella, Anne and Mark Barnes, Leisa Douglas, and Hope and Drew Lindsay.

—Lyah B. LeFlore

THE WORLD IS MINE

INTRODUCING

BLUE

THE DREAMER REYNOLDS

HEAT

CHAPTER ONE

BLUE

**Thinkin' of a master plan
Cuz ain't nothin' but sweat inside my hand
—Eric B. & Rakim, "Paid in Full"**

Click . . . Click . . . Click . . . Click . . .

I was fixated on the slowly clicking hand on my watch dial, counting down the final ten minutes of fifth period . . . second by second. I tapped my foot as if in sync with some imaginary beat, scanning the room, row after row of intense faces, struggling to get through the last questions on the composition essay exam. I'd already finished the exam five minutes ago. Not to be arrogant, but tests just come easy for me. I'm nice like that.

Don't get me wrong. I'm far from the smartest cat around. My boy Collin's got that covered. I just think I have the uncanny ability to retain information under pressure. In other words, I cram like hell. Something my dad and I don't see eye to eye on. He thinks I don't take my future serious enough, but he's wrong. I think about my future every minute—hell, every second of the day. Just like now. The wheels in my brain are churning like mad as I watch this whole scene unfold.

It's actually a cross between amusing and perplexing. Why? Because I wonder what the real reward in all this is. I mean, I get that the natural order of things is that you go to school to get a great job, in hopes that ultimately you'll become successful, and maybe even get rich in the process. But dig this, is success really determined by a textbook?

I've been thinking about all this a lot lately. I see my father every day preparing for a trial, or under pressure about some new case, all buttoned up in his corporate uniform—signature Brooks Brothers blue suit and tie, and his trademark leather briefcase. He looks like all the other clones lining up for the Metro day after day. It's a mundane existence, in my opinion. That may be cool for him, but it's not my destiny. I think when it comes to the career you choose, you should be doing something you love and that makes you happy. Isn't that the real key to success? That's what I'm seeking.

Okay, so I'm not quite sure yet what exactly my destiny is. I'm working on that. What I do know is that me and my friends—and, hell, probably all the other students at my high school for that matter—are young, and hungry. Probably hungrier than our parents were in their wildest imaginations. We want it all, and "it" for the most part is to come up. Maybe even become famous in the process.

What twenty-first-century teenager do you know who doesn't want to be famous? And not necessarily by becoming some Oscar-winning actor or Grammy-winning singer or even an all-star athlete. No, what I'm talking about is notoriety, perhaps from curing cancer or developing some huge green technological breakthrough. The point is, with notoriety comes the "paper," the "cheddar," the "cash flow," the "C.R.E.A.M." That's right, in the immortal words of the Wu-Tang Clan, "Cash rules everything around me, dollar, dollar bills, y'all!" Except I don't want to wait. I want mine now!

The thought is almost intoxicating, isn't it? So the question becomes, how does one parlay all these exams, term papers, and hours upon hours of studying into something major? Success should ultimately be about doin' *you*, not what the establishment dictates.

"Time's up!" The sound of Mr. Richardson's crackly voice snapped me out of my momentary state of contemplation. "Please drop your papers on the lectern as you exit," he announced. Some of the other students were still making last-second frantic scribbles. I grabbed my backpack, which was hanging on the back of my chair, and proceeded to the front of the classroom with my finished exam in hand.

I felt my Sidekick buzz. It was Collin:

MEET ME OUT FRONT

I didn't drive Mom's ride to school today, so I was catching a ride home with him.

I placed my completed test paper on the lectern and headed toward the exit.

"Mr. Reynolds, do you mind waiting?" Mr. Richardson called out. Damn, just what I didn't need. I stopped and slowly turned back around. "I'd like to have a word with you," he said, peering over his reading glasses. I felt my Sidekick buzz again.

"I actually have an appointment, Mr. Richardson. Could I drop by before classes tomorrow?" I anxiously replied.

"It'll only take a minute." He nodded, motioning for me to have a seat in a nearby chair as he sat down behind his desk.

"Is something wrong?" I asked.

"I noticed you finished the test early, as usual. Impressive," he said, scanning my test paper. "As a matter of fact, you always seem to do exceptionally well on your exams. If only you showed that same enthusiasm when it came to turning in homework assignments. I will say your test scores always save you when it's grading time." He pulled out a folder, flipping through the pages inside. "But what's most interesting, Mr. Reynolds, is that I've noticed that you seem to make a lot of references to music and pop culture in your writing. Is there any reason for that?"

"Well, sir, I really dig music. It's universal and influences literature. And as far as pop culture, it's all about connecting current trends and issues to the past to know where you're going." He looked as if he was going to explode after hearing my response. My Sidekick buzzed yet again.

"Mr. Reynolds, perhaps you find our curriculum boring."

"I wouldn't necessarily say boring, sir. Maybe I'm just preoccupied thinking about my future," I replied. There was an awkward silence.

"Interesting," he noted flatly. "Mr. Reynolds," he said, clearing his throat and taking a long pause before leaning in and removing his glasses. "You have the potential to be one of my brightest students, but you're also one of my most complicated. Therefore, that *future* that you're referring to can begin or end here at Silver Spring High. That depends on whether you pass all of your classes. What are your college plans?"

"I'm considering Morehouse College, or maybe even Syracuse, but my father wants me to go to Howard University, where he attended. Honestly, I haven't thought much about it, sir. I'm just a junior, and I figured I could think about that maybe next year," I said.

"Most of your peers are already talking about college, SATs, ACTs, early admission. I realize you're a junior, but senior year will zoom by, I can assure you. I'm going to recommend that you speak with Mr. Jones in the college and counseling office. Maybe he can give you some direction and motivation to participate a bit more in my class," he said, looking back down at my paper as if the words were about to miraculously jump off the page and do a trick. "I'd like for him to read your work as well."

I tossed him one of those yeah-sure-man-whatever looks. I was definitely not trying to feel this pressure right now. Did he not understand the meaning of "I have an appointment"? He was killing me right now, just like my buzzing Sidekick. I stole a quick peek at the screen. It was Collin again. I was sure he was heated by now, wondering where the hell I was. The message flashed:

SERIOUSLY DUDE!

"Um, Mr. Richardson, I'm sorry, but I really can't be late to that *appointment*." I stressed the word "appointment," hoping he'd get the message this time. "Is there anything else?"

"No. You're dismissed, Mr. Reynolds. I'll have Mr. Jones in the counseling office contact you," he said.

He didn't need to tell me twice. I made a mad dash out of that classroom, down the hallway, and into the school's atrium. I didn't slow down until I knew I was in the clear. The atrium was the large foyer-like area at Silver Spring High, or SSH as we all call it, where everyone congregated before and after classes. It was crowded as usual with the after-school pockets of crews and chick cliques.

As I passed through, headed for the exit, I gave out pounds, whassups, and hugs to a couple of the girls. SSH is really no different from most suburban high schools in America. You got your preps, nerds, jocks, the cool kids, and the girls, aka the shorties and the honeys. I'm down with everybody, especially the latter. "Respect and love to all" is my motto. I can't even imagine fighting or beefing with anybody. That's just not cool.

"Blue!" A sugary voice chirped from behind.

"Oh, hey. Whassup, Christine," I said, leaning in to kiss her on the cheek. "You good?"

"Yeah, but," she said, then pulling me close, "I thought you were going to call me." She winked.

"My bad. I, um, lost my cell." I was searching desperately for a viable excuse. Christine, aka Sex Fiend Christine, ran her fingers seductively across my chest, as I struggled to come up with more excuses. Collin pulled up in front just in time. On the real, Christine was a sweet girl, but not my type at all. I'm definitely not into the nip/tuck babes. Babygirl went from an A-cup to a double D over the summer. Word is she even had one of those Brazilian booty jobs. Nah, I'm strictly into the all-natural, if you know what I mean.

Collin blasted his horn and waved out the driver's window.

"Dude!" he yelled with a twisted expression.

"A-yo! I'm comin'!" I shouted, tossing up the peace sign. I turned back to Christine. "Yo, you know I'm just focused on school right now, babygirl, but I'll get at you." I quickly pecked her on the cheek again, making a smooth escape, leaving Christine in a huff.

I jumped into the passenger seat of Collin's SUV, and we gave each other a round of pounds. For damn near my whole life Collin and I have been tight. We're practically brothers.

Our dads worked for the same judge when they were rookie lawyers.

"You're killing me, dude. I've been waiting out here forever, man," Collin said, slipping on his aviators and slamming the car into drive. Collin was that preppy but fly type guy with an Abercrombie & Fitch catalog vibe.

"My bad. Mr. Richardson held me up. However, nice save from Sex Fiend Christine."

"Look, if you want me to hang tonight, then I've gotta get home and get some serious studying in. Big psych exam next week. I'm not like you. I don't subscribe to the cram method."

"Yo, C, you really need to take something for all that stressful energy," I said, shaking my head. "You need to chill, *relax* sometimes."

"I've got the fix right here," he said, giving a sly grin. "Time for a bit of fellowship!" Collin inconspicuously flashed the freshly rolled blunt tucked in his jacket pocket. The term "fellowship" was another word for smoking weed. Smoking wasn't really my thing, but to each his own.

Minutes later, we were slowly turning down the road leading into Rock Creek Park. It was the biggest park in DC and only ten minutes away from SSH. A lot of cats from school come here to hang out, and on the low, mainly to smoke weed or chill with their girls. This is definitely a good "low, low" spot to hit on date nights. Collin pulled into an empty lot, put the car in park, and wasted no time firing up the blunt. After he took a deep inhale, he motioned the blunt in my direction.

"Nah, I'm straight," I said, selecting a track on Collin's iPod, which was hooked up to the car's stereo. I leaned back in my seat, sinking into the base line. "I don't know why you smoke that stuff."

"Because, dude, it's like de-stressing at its finest," Collin said, letting out a big cloud of smoke. "Whiteboy hooked me up with some fantastic herbals this time, for sure." He took another puff. Whiteboy was our other homeboy and had the hookup on everything from weed and rims to DVDs of the latest box-office flicks, and cool sneakers that weren't even sold in the regular stores. He didn't sell drugs or anything, but let's just say he was "connected."

"Shit's been insanely hectic. I'm waiting on my SAT test scores. My dad is all over me about them," he said, tapping the ash off the tip of the blunt.

"Yo, I don't know why you took it so soon. We've got a whole year before graduation and all that. Your pops be sweatin' you like crazy. Whassup with that?" I said.

"Hey, I'm used to the pressure. My dad doesn't give me a freakin' break. Besides, if you want to get into the best schools, you've gotta test as many times as you can and apply early."

"You push yourself too much, C," I said, shaking my head.

"Yeah, right. Whatever, dude. Coming from a man who barely studies for tests and aces those shits! That's crazy. Meanwhile, some of us have to bust ass on the books," he said.

"Yeah, but you don't even need to. Your dad can just make a call. Besides, you'll probably get a perfect score on that SAT. Your testing skills are outta here."

"I'd better, after all those SAT and ACT prep courses, and the litany of AP courses. Look, call or no call from my dad, he's riding me hard about attending his alma mater, Georgetown," he said, taking a final long pull on the blunt, closing his eyes, and holding the smoke in.

My boy Collin had all the makings in his pristine background to be "that" dude. His father's money and connections were at the top of the list. The Andrewses' pockets are deep. His grandfather's relationships are even rooted in Washington politics. His dad is a lawyer, and so is my dad, but let's keep it real, my dad's connections don't compare to the Andrews name. That's just the socioeconomic structure of things. Bottom line, my family just doesn't have it like that. But what makes Collin so cool, and why I give him his props, is that he's never taken being born with a silver spoon in his mouth for granted. Plus, he and his family have had their share of drama in recent years. Like Diddy's famous line, "Mo money, mo problems."

"C, I just want you to remember that life is too short. What about what *you* want? I'm realizing that it's more about what's going to make *me* happy. That's more important than what my pops wants. You only get one go-round. You feel me?"

"You try telling my dad that crap." He coughed, letting out a puff of smoke, slowly backing out of the parking spot.

"Check it out. I keep having this crazy dream," I said, changing the subject.

"Dream about what?" he said as we cruised through the park. "Are you sure you didn't catch a crazy contact high back there?" he said, and laughed.

"I'm serious. Listen, in it I'm always with some big music star, like Jay-Z, Diddy, Kanye, or Usher, somebody like that. The cast of superstars keeps changing, but that's irrelevant. The point is, I'm always in this car riding, and not just any car, but a white convertible Phantom."

"Sweet!" Collin said as he high-fived me with his free hand.

"Okay, so, I'm in the driver's seat and in a serious exchange, but I can never make out what exactly we're talking about. I just know it's business."

"Yeah, dude, you're definitely flying high!" Collin snickered again. "Doo, doo, doo, doo," he mocked to the tune of *The Twilight Zone* theme.

"Yo, for real, chill!" I said with intensity.

"Okay, okay. Keep going," he said as we continued driving.

"It's like I'm a confidant to these people or something, and they're listening to me. So, last night Lil Wayne was in the dream and we're riding down 495 in this badass Phantom. I could see the DC skyline in the rearview mirror. Where we were headed, I don't know. I noticed we were the only people on the highway, just me and Lil Wayne. The top was down and the sun was blinding.

"He turned to me and in a surreal moment said, 'I heard

you got it.' I was confused. 'Got what?' I said back to him. He gave a sly laugh, transmitting a menacing look behind his dark shades, chuckling once more. 'You got *it*. You the truth, B. Just get ready.' So I ask, 'Get ready for what?' And he says, 'To blow up!' Then he leaned his head back on the headrest, and on the side of his face there was a tattoo. It read 'Choson.' Then I put my foot on the gas and we zoomed off. That was it. That was the end of the dream. Get it? Cho-*son*. Like *chosen*!"

By the time I finished telling Collin about the dream, we were parked in front of my house.

"Wow, that was the deepest shit I've ever heard," Collin said, unlocking the doors. "I mean, I'm buzzed, but that took my high to another level."

"I think it means I need to find my real hook in life. Once I find that hook, I'm outta here!"

"Dude, c'mon, though. I got respect for you, but you can't be serious about putting your future on a dream. Success happens when you have a plan. It's all about a plan, mapping it all out, you know? Working hard. I mean, I'm a realist," he said, removing his shades, raising his eyebrow.

"Yeah, but I believe in omens and signs and shit. Maybe the dream is a sign," I said, grabbing my bag and getting out. "I'm out!" I said, giving him a pound.

"I'll hit you after I study. 'Cause that's my guaranteed way to score *my* hook! Peace out, dude!" he said, throwing up the peace sign and shutting the car door.

As Collin pulled away, suddenly that same feeling I had in the dream was tugging on my gut. I stood in my driveway and thought, *Damn, what if the dream was confirmation that I was on the brink of something . . . something big, colossal even?*

INTRODUCING

COLLIN

ANDREWS

the Realist

CHAPTER TWO

COLLIN

I don't need no intermission
My life's in hi-definition
—Lupe Fiasco, "Hi-Definition"

By the time I made it home, my high had mellowed out. Unfortunately, the envelope with my SAT scores that greeted me in the mailbox further punctuated my buzz-free state. Reality sucked. I placed the envelope on the corner of my desk and stared at it. I know Blue thinks I'm too uptight about tests, grades, college, all of it, but he doesn't understand.

While he dreams about Lil Wayne and Jay-Z, I go to bed dreaming about things like getting a perfect 2400 on the SAT, or graduating class valedictorian, or even making Law Review my first year of law school. I could feel a knot forming in the back of my neck. I rolled my shoulders to knock it out. I thought the whole point of blazing up was to escape.

Note to self: *Tell Whiteboy I need an upgrade on the herbal medicinals next time.* I leaned back in my chair, clasping my fingers behind my head, and let out a deep breath.

The full moon reflected off the quietly rippling water in the swimming pool below my bedroom window. My father was downstairs in his study, probably on his second or third Jack and Coke. The house was eerily quiet, as usual. Honestly, I never wanted to move here. After everything happened, my dad decided to take over my grandfather's firm, Andrews, Weinberger, and Taub. To do so we had to come back to Maryland. My dad grew up in DC. It actually hasn't been so bad living here for the past few years. The worst part was leaving my mother. I didn't want her to be alone, but she felt it was best for me to be with my dad after the divorce.

It's funny, I was born in this house, and we left and moved to New York when I was five. It's always been here, but I never thought we'd come back to live in it again. Not like this. It's just a *house*, not a *home*. What the hell did two people need with five bedrooms and nearly six thousand square feet, anyway? They say a man's home is his castle—in this case, his fortress.

Chevy Chase, Maryland, had real estate with million-dollar-plus price tags. But hey, in a world where your dad is one of the most powerful lawyers in Washington DC, material gain, power, privilege, and name recognition come with the territory. It might sound crazy to you, but sometimes I wish I could trade my life with Blue's. At least he and his father communicate.

I considered sparking up another blunt. Then I realized I had smoked my last one. Fan-freakin'-tastic! Just then my cell rang. The caller ID flashed MOM. I hesitated answering. That probably sounds messed up, but I just didn't know if I could deal today. I love my mom, but it sucks that I'm in the middle of things between her and my dad. My phone rang again. I pressed talk.

"How's my favorite future Georgetown legal eagle?" she greeted.

"Yeah, well I don't know about the Georgetown part. We don't want to jump the gun," I said, and laughed.

"It's in your blood, Collin." We shared a laugh. "Anyway, I don't want to bother you. I was just thinking about you," she said softly, then paused. "I miss you, Collin."

"You okay, Mom? I mean, is everything all right?"

"I'm fine. I actually like it out here much better than the city."

"I miss you too, Mom, and you could never bother me."

"Maybe during Christmas break you could come up."

"Sure. We could sing carols around the fire just like old times."

"And I could bake your favorite—sugar cookies," she said. I could feel the smile across her face.

"I can't wait until summer, either. The parties in the Hamptons are the best. Blue and I could come out." I gave a half smile. "I'll be able to breathe by then. I've been swamped at school and with early college prep stuff, but everything's great."

"Just please promise me that you'll find time to enjoy yourself too. You're young. You have your whole life ahead of you. Please. I'm so proud of you, Collin. I'm sure your father is too." I could suddenly hear a sense of sadness in her voice.

"The jury's still out on that one," I said, picking up the envelope and holding it up to the light, before flicking it across the room. "Dad's head is so far up his—"

"Don't say that!" She sternly cut me off. "Your father wasn't always like this, Collin. . . ." Her voice softly trailed off.

Since everything happened, and the split four years ago, my mom has really had a hard time adjusting to things. Sure, I worry about her. It's like nobody—her or my dad—is dealing with reality. Why should I? I'm glad she moved out to the Hamptons. It was for the best. She spent most of her childhood there. Staying in New York City would've been too much. There were too many memories . . . for all of us.

"Mom, I just want you to get better. Dad doesn't realize what he lost. Please, Mom, try not to worry so much about me. I'm fine. But I've gotta go. I need to study. Blue and I are hangin' out tonight."

"I love you, Collin."

"Love you, too."

I disconnected the call and stared for a long time at the envelope across the room that would determine my future or demise. I was too nervous to open it. The label read TO THE ATTENTION OF MR. COLLIN JACOB ANDREWS II." I was named after my father, *Attorney* Collin Jacob Andrews. What a joke. I was nothing like him. *Just get it over with, dude,* I told myself, picking up the envelope again, examining it closer. It was practically burning a hole through my hand.

What's that saying? There's nothing to fear but fear itself. More like, there's no fear like the fear of failing in the eyes of my father. Just once I'd like to really show him! I slowly placed the envelope in my desk drawer. Maybe tomorrow. I shook it off and opened my psychology book, forgetting about the envelope for now.

Two hours later my brain was fried and I welcomed a break from the books. I took a quick shower; changed into some jeans, loafers, a dress shirt, and blazer; grabbed my wallet and keys; and exited my room. I poked my head into my dad's study downstairs. As suspected he was downing a glass of Jack and Coke, reading over some files.

"Hey, Dad? I'm headed out to meet up with Blue. There's a blackout party at school."

"I hope you and your buddy Blue score as high on your

placement exams as you score at parties. Georgetown certainly won't care about your social rating," he said coldly, never even looking up from his papers.

My jaw tightened and I gripped the keys in my hand firmly. "I've been studying really hard. I'm just going out to let off some steam."

"You missed the point, Collin. You've been studying, but what are the results? Until you get into Georgetown, you have no results, and the hard work doesn't stop there," he said, peering over his reading glasses. I let out an exasperated sigh. "Collin, my job is to push you. When I was in my junior and senior years of high school, a day didn't go by that I wasn't focused on my studies. We've seen what losing focus can do in this family," he said with disdain.

"My years at Georgetown were the best years of my life. I graduated at the top of my class, made Law Review consecutive years, and passed the bar with flying colors. That's what you should be aspiring to do. I could've gone right into the family firm, but I rolled up my sleeves and worked in New York first. It's about your work ethic, son. That's what the top firms like Andrews, Weinberger, and Taub look at. Your grandfather founded one of the best."

"Yes, sir," I said through gritted teeth. I was ready to explode, but it wouldn't do any good. My father's ears don't hear my voice. Fuck this! I bolted.

I texted Blue:

ON MY WAY

Sunroof open, feeling the wind whip around me, Lupe Fiasco blastin' was the remedy.

Hip-hop just saved my life. . . .

CHAPTER THREE

BLUE

As I recall I know you love to show off
But I never thought that you would take it this far
—Kanye West, "Flashing Lights"

Collin and I glided through the throng of people standing out-side the SSH gym waiting to get in.

"Yo, what's the problem? What's the hold up?" I asked, tap-ping the guy in front of us on the back. He shrugged his shoul-ders and turned around.

"Dude, I could've still been studying," Collin said, agitated. "This is so lame!"

"No. What's wack is that they're not letting anybody in," I said.

"Speaking of wack, where's Whiteboy? He's always late, dude," Collin said, shaking his head.

I pulled out my Sidekick and typed in a quick text:

WHERE U AT FOOL?

The line was finally starting to move. Blackout parties were some of the best parties at the local high schools. I usually preferred the club parties on teen nights, but when it was a blackout joint, you didn't want to miss out. Once a month a school in the area hosted it, and they hired a local Go Go band and a popular local deejay, and everyone came and rocked out. Tonight SSH had one of the best Go Go bands in town playing, TCB.

Go Go is the trademark sound of this part of the country. The DC metro area made it famous. Just like how New York laid the foundation for hip-hop. Go Go is all about heavy percussion and live instruments. Sometimes the band will mix an old-school song with a funk flavor, and damn, the crowd goes nuts. Plus the girls go crazy when they hear it.

"A-yo!" Collin and I turned around to see Whiteboy dashing across the parking lot toward us. "What's poppin', young!" He said, giving us each a pound. "Young" is a friendly slang term we use to refer to each other sometimes. Like brotherly endearment. It's definitely a DC and Maryland thing!

"I had a cat come in right at closing and he wanted me to touch up his tat," he said.

Whiteboy is the sickest tattoo artist in PG County. Everybody from NBA and NFL ballplayers to rebellious suburban kids, even local hustlers, come and get their tats done in his chair at Cutz and Tatz. It's a cool barbershop in Adams Morgan, not too far from Silver Spring and my neighborhood. I get my hair cut there weekly, and Whiteboy runs a tattoo booth inside the shop.

"By default you made it just in time. Looks like the party is about to get started," I said, making note that the line was finally moving. "I'm hyped to check out TCB!"

"They're tight!" Collin added.

"Damn, I see that cornball Jerard is working the door," Whiteboy said, pointing toward the front of the line.

"You still have that kid shook from two years ago!" I joked. "Remember when he told Dr. Thompson, our old principal, that you were the one who set off the fire alarms?"

"Dude, when you were at SSH, it was mayhem on a daily basis. People would part the halls like the Red Sea when you came through," Collin said, giving Whiteboy a high five.

"I couldn't go with that school flow. Too many rules."

"Dude, you had a fight like every day for the two months you were here at SSH," Collin said.

"Word, that's when I used to wild out! On the real, sometimes I think maybe I should've never quit, but shit happens, right?"

"Hey, I give you props. You had my back that time those cats from Northeast tried to step to me and Collin in the parking lot after homecoming."

"No doubt. I remembered when C let me cheat off that history exam. It was the *one* test I've passed in my whole life!" Whiteboy gave us each another round of high fives.

Whiteboy is like the *realest* cat I've ever met. Don't let his skin color fool you. That dude's harder than most cats from the worst parts of DC. He's from Baltimore, or B-more, as we call it. The straight-up streets of B-more too. He grew up gangbangin', stealin' cars, blah, blah, blah. Basically, talk to his P.O. about the rest. He said for as long as he can remember everybody's been calling him Whiteboy. I guess the nickname just stuck. He's two years older than us, but has already spent much of his life in and out of juvie hall. He gets respect in the hood because he came up hard.

"Whatever you do, just play it cool at the door, Whiteboy," Collin warned. "After all this time we've waited in line, I'm not trying to get tossed out before we get in. Plus, you know Jerard is still traumatized from what you did to him."

"Five dollars each *and* your student ID," Jerard demanded. I collected five dollars from Collin and Whiteboy and handed fifteen to Jerard.

"*And* student IDs!" Jerard snapped, eyeing Whiteboy.

"Man, fuck this party and this punk-ass busta!" Whiteboy said, grabbing a trembling Jerard by the collar. "I should've left you hangin' on that lamppost, fool!" Guffaws and snickers erupted from people standing behind us as well as other party-goers ready to instigate trouble.

"Cool out, Whiteboy!" I said, pushing him back and smoothing down Jerard's collar.

"Blue, I'm in charge of student government, and I don't want any trouble!" Jerard shouted, breaking out in a sweat.

"I know, and we got respect for you, but c'mon, Jerard, stop hatin'" I said. Collin and I both knew it was best to keep tempers cool. Whiteboy definitely had a short fuse.

"I got your ID, punk ass!" Whiteboy chided, grabbing his crotch.

"Chill!" I said through a clenched jaw. Jerard rolled his eyes and reluctantly took the money. I let out a sigh of relief.

"Yo, I was just playin' with you, homie." Whiteboy flashed a playful grin and patted Jerard on the shoulder.

"Dude, you're gonna give him a heart attack one of these days," Collin said, shaking his head as we continued into the school's gym.

"C'mon, C, I was just havin' some fun," Whiteboy said, and snickered.

Once we were inside the party, the scene was a major disappointment. Everyone was standing around. No one was dancing, and the deejay was playing all the wrong music. Britney Spears is a definite *N-O*!

"Negative, dude. This is a bust. I demand a refund!" Collin said, throwing up his arms.

"Yeah, but look at all these people up in here. Maybe we didn't get the memo. They're makin' crazy paper off this joint!" The place was packed, but the people were more interested in texting and talking on their cells.

"Yo, and how wack is the hypeman standing next to the deejay?" I pointed toward the stage.

"Dude, I just overheard a few fools talking about tomorrow's lunch menu. I say we leave," Collin said, checking his watch.

The hypeman was trying his best to pump up the crowd by shouting, "Let's get it started!" into the mic. It was a lost cause. Moments later, a flustered Jerard raced past. I grabbed him by the arm, stopping him in his tracks. "Yo, Jerard, whassup with the clown onstage?" I asked.

"The band, TCB, is late and the deejay sucks. I don't have time to talk!" Jerard rushed off in panic mode.

"Let's bounce!" Whiteboy shouted over the music.

The party had all of the right elements: hot girls, a great venue, and even sexy lighting for a school gym, but the wack level was at an all-time high because it was missing that "spark." Someone who could ignite the crowd.

"If this was my joint, I would have the crowd rockin' like Diddy!" I said.

"Anyone could do better than this guy," Collin said, cutting me a look.

"That's what I'm sayin'! It's about bringing out the energy in a room. One person *can* do that!" I said, suddenly pumping myself up. "I ought to show him how it's done."

"Dude, you're scaring me. Please don't tell me you're serious," Collin said with a raised eyebrow.

"Then, playa, you talkin' all that trash, get yo ass up there and do somethin', 'cause I see some ladies tonight that should be havin' my baby . . . bay-BAY!" Whiteboy said, imitating the Notorious B.I.G.'s famous line. He gave Collin a pound.

The wheels in my head started churning and it was like something came over me. I got that feeling in my gut, and before anyone could stop me, I hopped onstage and whispered to the deejay to put on some of that classic Kanye.

When the base line of "Flashing Lights" dropped, I stepped to the stunned cornball hypeman and grabbed the mic, ordering everyone to report to the dance floor. Then I told the deejay to rewind the track one more time. I started waving my arms in the air, and my boys, Collin and Whiteboy, were front and center waving right along with me. The crowd started chanting "Go, Blue! Get busy!" At that point I lost it and broke it down with the latest dance move. I was in a zone.

After the deejay played the record a couple more times, the band, TCB, slid onstage and started jammin' with a live Go Go version of "Flashing Lights." For a moment, I stood looking out over the sea of people. A euphoric feeling washed over me. I handed the mic back to the wack hypeman and jumped off the stage. As me and my crew walked through the crowd, headed toward the exit, high fives and major props were coming from everyone in the room. Perhaps tonight a "supastar" was born!

The next day, I decided to get in some study time. My mom was so ecstatic, I think she peeked in my room at least four times to make sure her eyes weren't deceiving her. They weren't, but I ain't lyin', it was hard to focus, because I was still on a high from taking the stage at the blackout party. My Sidekick hadn't stopped buzzing with messages like "When's your next party?" and "Congrats on a hot joint, playboy!"

Collin sent a new text:

WE BALLIN.

I typed back:

HELL YEAH!

That's all I needed to call an official study time-out. I grabbed my sneaks and raced down the steps, two at a time. Collin and Whiteboy were already at the park hoopin'. I scooped up my basketball before darting past my mom, who was standing in the living room wiping her hands on a dish towel.

"Slow down, mister, and stop bouncing that ball in my house!" she said, giving me a swat on the back.

"My bad, Mom!" I said, giving her a quick peck on the cheek.

"I thought you were studying. And kisses won't fix what you break with that ball!"

"I was and it won't"—kiss—"happen"—kiss—"again." Kiss. Kiss. Kiss. "Promise!"

"Blue! Dinner's at six. Don't be late," she warned.

"I got you!" I winked, snatching the spare keys to her car off the hall table and jetting out the front door.

"Blue Jamal Reynolds, you'd better put gas in my car!" she called out, one final warning.

"Yes, ma'am!" I flashed a smile, threw up the peace sign, and winked again as I backed out of the driveway. I hit play on my iPod, which was connected to the car's sound system. The thump of the base line from an old-school Tupac track pumped through the car speakers. I nodded my head as if on cue. My cell buzzed, and I pressed speaker.

"Speak!" I said, shouting into the phone.

"Whassup, playboy! Where you at? You must be frontin', 'cause you know I'm gonna school that asssssss!" Whiteboy was always talkin' smack. I laughed.

"C'mon, *supastar*, so I can shut you down!" Collin chimed in.

"Yo, C, I don't want to kill your dream, but you couldn't take me out if LeBron was your personal trainer. Be there in ten!" I laughed, pressed end, and hit the volume, cruising down East-West Highway.

When I pulled up to the park, Collin and Whiteboy were playing one-on-one. I parked, hopped out, and jogged over to the court. I gave each of them a pound.

"Oh, my God! Heads have been blowin' me up with text messages all morning." I beamed.

"Man, me too! Last night was freakin' great!" Collin said, excitedly giving me a high five.

"You know you rocked that shit, B!" Whiteboy noted, passing the ball to Collin.

"I wish I could've made that paper, though," I noted.

"Thas whassup!" Whiteboy said, giving me a pound.

"I've gotta admit, you had me nervous at first," Collin said.

"So you're admitting you've seen the light?" I bragged.

"Yeah, yeah, okay, I'll give you your props for last night's display of greatness onstage, but let's get on with this beatin'," Collin said, shooting the ball, missing the hoop by a mile.

"C, now, you know you white boys can't ball like the brothas! Every twenty years or so you get a Larry Bird or a Steve Nash, but you know the deal. Black rules the blacktop!" I joked.

"Nah, young, me and C ain't in the same category! I guess I'mma have to break both of y'all off a li'l somethin' somethin'!" Whiteboy said, catching the rebound, setting up the layup, and then dunking the ball in the hoop.

"My bad. You don't count, Whiteboy. You ain't really white!" I joked.

"Aw, young, how you gon' play me out like that?" Whiteboy smirked. "Don't hate 'cause I got skills!" Whiteboy removed his shirt and started flexing his muscles.

"Aw, dude, I'm gonna be sick," Collin said, faking like he was nauseous. "Thanks for sharing your little four-pack." He gave Whiteboy a shove.

"Whatever! Alls I got ta say is 'Hi, hater!'" Whiteboy teased, waving his hand in the air.

"Yo, I'm with C. Ain't no chicks out here," I said, giving Collin a pound. "No, seriously, nice tat."

"Both of y'all are haters, and for the record it's a *six*-pack," Whiteboy said, and flashed a toothy smile. "And I'm glad you like the new tat. Stop jockin'! I'm tryin' to let it breathe," he said, showing off a large colorful tattoo emblazoned across the side of his rib cage. It was a drawing of a heart with angel wings coming out of it and "Grandma Rose" written in script across it.

"I did it in memory of my grandmother. Out of all my other tats," he said, pointing to an intricate serpent on his left leg and his ornately covered arms, "this one's the most special. My boy down in B-more who did this new one hooked me up. Tight, right?"

"I don't know how you tolerate the pain," Collin said, squinting at the new tat.

"Grandma Rose was the only person who ever had my back," he said, wiping the sweat from his face with his T-shirt, then slipping it back on.

"You must love her, 'cause the rib cage is the most painful area to get one of those," I said.

"I've seen fools throw up when I try to tat them up on the ribs. But, hey, she was my heart, so I had to endure that pain, feel me? Word up," he said, getting misty-eyed.

"Hold up, are those tears?" Collin teased.

"I didn't know thugs were so sensitive," I said, running after the ball, tossing it back to Whiteboy.

"What can I say? Thugs need love too!" Whiteboy said, dribbling.

Me and my crew were always talking trash, joking around, especially on the basketball court, but we definitely have each other's backs.

"Oh, by the way, just givin' you fools a heads-up," Whiteboy said. "I'm picking up my new ride in a few days. I've been savin' for it."

"You got it!" I said, giving him a pound.

"Candy paint, Mustang! Off the hiz-zook!" he boasted.

"Sweet!" Collin added.

I dribbled over to a nearby picnic bench and sat down. Collin and Whiteboy joined me. I pulled out my Sidekick and started scrolling through my new messages. "Hey, C, did you get the test scores you were waiting for yet?" I asked.

"Nah," Collin replied.

"Man, I haven't even taken the practice SAT yet. My pops is driving me crazy about going up to visit his alma mater, Howard, too. But don't trip. You know you're gonna get a perfect score," I said, tossing him the ball.

"If you say so, dude," Collin said, catching it and dribbling it in place.

"Check this out, Whiteboy!" A message caught my attention. "Jerard, your buddy from student government, just sent me a message asking me to host the homecoming festivities next week!"

"Are you serious? That's hot!" Collin high-fived me.

"Word up!" Whiteboy added.

"I think I wanna do it," I said.

"Yeah, but what do you get out of it? Are you getting paid? What kind of perks?" Collin asked.

"Fool, all the chicks will be on his jock. That's what he'll get!" Whiteboy snatched the ball and did a smooth between-the-legs dribble.

"You're insane! No. C's got a point," I said, nodding toward Collin. "My man! Your business sense is on point."

"Hey, I'm just saying get the details!" Collin added. "You just need to make sure you benefit from doing it."

"I'm with you. I'm gonna find out my benefits, and then let him know I'm down," I said, giving Whiteboy a pound.

"Wait a minute, Blue, before you hit him back. Let me play devil's advocate for a minute. What if you just got lucky last night?" Collin questioned.

"Aw, damn, you're like the dark cloud, playboy! I say go for yours, B! Screw that devil's advocate crap," Whiteboy said, waving Collin off.

"*Lucky?* C'mon. Last night was too dope to be classified as lucky. What about the dreams I've been having?"

"What dreams, B?" Whiteboy chuckled.

"Blue, they're just dreams," Collin said, throwing his hands into the air.

"Whatever, man! Look, I keep having these dreams about blowing up in the music business. Maybe last night's party was confirmation. Maybe it was that hook I need. I'm gonna hit Jerard back now before he gets somebody else!" I said.

"Obviously you're set on doing this. Just remember to ask what he's offering—money, advertisement, something!" Collin stressed again.

"I'm on it!" I quickly typed in a text to Jerard. Within seconds he shot back a response. "He's offering one-fifty!" I said, looking at my Sidekick screen.

"Hells, no! That ain't no real paper," Whiteboy interjected.

I was about to tell Jerard to forget it when Collin stopped me. "Both of you chill out! Blue, do you really want this?"

"Yeah, I feel like I could be building a rep here."

"Well, there's no denying what you did last night, and if you believe this is in fact your hook, then take the money he's offering as a onetime deal. Make the party bigger and better. As a matter of fact, make it the best homecoming SSH has ever seen," Collin said, nodding his head. He was definitely digging the idea.

"So, I make it seem like *he's* getting a deal, a discounted rate, like I'm lookin' out for him and the school. I know and you all know that this is still about proving myself. But I'm cool with that. I ain't never been scared of a challenge."

"Exactly!" Collin snatched my Sidekick and started texting away. By the time Collin and I finished working out the details, Jerard's final offer was the one-fifty, plus my photo on all the promotion and advertisement. Whiteboy even volunteered to do the graphic layouts. I was going to win big, and I had just one week before I was set to rock the house.

"I get it! Sometimes it's about looking at the bigger picture," I said, giving Collin a pound.

"Yo, B, you might mess around and be like that cat Rico Tate," Whiteboy said, holding up the ball.

"*The* Rico Tate, who owns half the clubs in DC? I wish. His latest spot is that new tri-level joint, Club Heat!" I said.

"Yeah, he comes to the shop to get his hair cut sometimes. Dre, the owner, mostly goes to him. I even gave his security dude a tat," Whiteboy added.

"Yeah, I could be like that dude!" I was hyped. "It's time to get this!" I said, grabbing the ball and shooting it from half-court. *Swish!* "Nothin' but net!"

"Lucky shot!" Collin shouted, running to catch the rebound.

"And the crowd goes wild!" I shouted, striking an old-school b-boy pose. *One day you're gonna be famous, son!* I thought, smiling to myself.

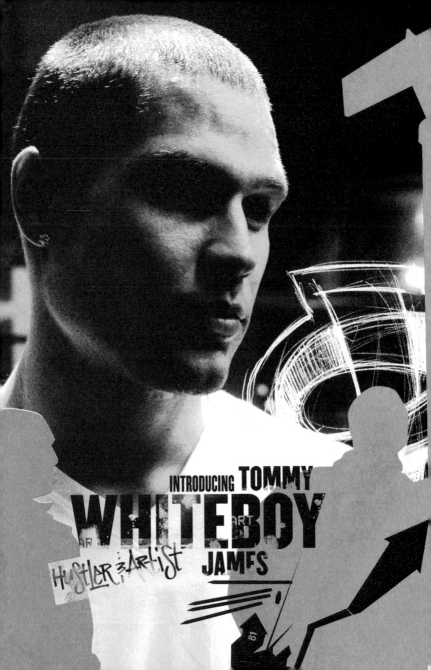

INTRODUCING TOMMY
WHITEBOY
Hustler & Artist JAMES

CHAPTER FOUR

WHITEBOY

Do you have any clue what I had to do to get here?
—Jay-Z featuring Eminem, "Renegade"

Collin slowed to a stop in front of 202 Dubs, the hot car spot where all the ballers who want to hook up their whips come. I've seen some sick rides roll out of here, wood grain dashboard, Gucci and Louis Vuitton printed interiors, the works. But flash ain't never really been my style. My face was lit up like a five-year-old's at Christmastime. Collin looked over at me and started laughing his ass off.

"Yo, what's funny, C?"

"You, dude. You're really geeked about this car, huh?" Collin asked.

"I ain't gonna even front. I'm crazy hyped," I said with a big cheeseburger smile plastered across my face. "When I was a shortie in juvie, I saw a picture of this car, and I never thought I'd get one like it. Blue's talkin' about *his* dreams, man. It's like *my* dreams are coming true. I guess I can relate to how he feels."

We parked and walked up to the garage's entrance, where my homeboy Juice, the owner, was working under the hood of a car.

"Man, this place is like a real-life *Pimp My Ride*," Collin said.

"Word. Juice is the real deal. He was like a big brother to me when I was in juvie. He actually was the one who talked some sense into my head. He's a few years older so he's seen a lot." The garage's sound system was blasting some cool old-school hip-hop. "Juicy Juice!" I called out over the music. Juice removed his work goggles and flashed one of his famous gold-filled smiles. He hit the remote to the stereo, turning the music down.

"Whassup, playboy!" Juice gave me a pound. He was as big as a linebacker.

"Juice, this is my boy Collin."

"Peace, li'l homie." He gave Collin a pound. "So you ready?"

"Ready as I'm gonna get. Man, I'm nervous, but in a good way," I said.

He walked us over to a covered car and in a quick move yanked the cover off. I couldn't believe my eyes. Juice had turned an old rusted-out '65 Mustang into the hottest set of wheels rollin' on these streets.

"Juice, you hooked your boy up!" I said in amazement.

"Always. You know I had to come wit it for you, youngblood. You ain't gotta dream no more, baby! I don't know if your man Collin knows how far we go back, but it's deep. See, Collin, youngblood here didn't pick his circumstances. Life just happens like that sometimes. Ya feel me?" Juice was getting ready to speak, as he calls it, the "truth."

Collin shook his head, soaking it all in. I don't know if he was ready for the knowledge Juice was about to drop. We all walked over to the car to admire it closer.

"I've come a long way from the streets, but I saw talent and potential in Whiteboy from day one. Remember, li'l homie, when you came up in juvie all hard, fightin' anybody who got in your way? It was like you were tryin' to prove you were a gangsta." Juice laughed.

"I was lost, but when I met Juice, I saw how much respect he was getting and I wanted that respect too. So I asked him," I said.

"And that's when I told him about my life and about coming from nothing. I had just read a book called *Manchild in the Promised Land*. I understood that cats like my pops were broken by the system. He ran because he was scared. He couldn't show me how to be a man. What I thought was being a man was really being a dumb boy. I made a choice right then and there that I wasn't going to waste my talent on stealin' cars, but use it to rebuild them. I could make other people happy for a change with these hands, instead of hurtin' them. Feel me?" He looked down at his hands. "I wasn't going to let my father's life dictate my life."

"You cool, C? Juice didn't come too heavy for you, did he?" I noticed that Juice's words had affected Collin, but I wasn't going to press.

"Yeah, yeah, I'm cool," he said, clearing his throat.

"I'm sorry, Whiteboy, but you know me. I can't open my mouth and not speak it," he said, patting me on the back. "Youngblood, you got crazy talent, and that's why I went the extra distance with the woofers and tweeters, and put these hot 22s on this ride."

"Yo, this is great, Juice, but I ain't really got the cash to pay for them right now. I mean, I can get it, but it's gonna take me a little time—"

"Hold up," Juice cut me off. "These wheels and this sound system are my gift to you. You did my sign for free, and my tat of my mother when she passed away a year ago," he said, raising his sleeve to show off the elaborate tattoo I had drawn. "Nuff said! Check it out, voilà!" Juice pulled off the paper taped over the doors.

"Oh, snap! Hells, no! This is crazy, fly, ridiculous, stupid, ignorant, off the hook!" I shouted, jumping around. It was almost an exact replica of the tattoo on my rib cage, except my grandma's name wasn't written on it. My grandma's eyes were etched in the wings.

"How did you do this?" I asked excitedly.

"Remember when you drew that picture and gave it to me the day I got out? I kept it all this time," Juice said.

"Yo, that's crazy! I just got a tattoo done of this same drawing. Thas whassup!"

"Sweet! Great work, Juice," Collin said. "Okay, Whiteboy, I gotta jet. Blue's gonna love the new ride. Oh, and by the way, get me those graphics for the homecoming posters and flyers. The school's gotta be plastered with them."

We gave each other pounds, and I pulled off shortly after Collin, but not before Juice called out, "Watch these DC haters, youngblood!"

I had mad pride driving down the DC streets. Where I came from, I never had much to look forward to. Feeling the steering wheel in my hands took me back to my own promise I made, kneeling at my dead grandma's grave before I left B-more. I told her that I would never sell drugs or rob or steal again. I would show the world my talent. I hope I never have to break that promise. I'm damn sure gonna try my best not to.

I slipped that classic Jay-Z CD, *The Blueprint*, in and skipped to the track featuring Eminem: "I'm just a kid from the gutter makin' this butter off these bloodsuckers 'cause I'm a renegade . . ."

My phone buzzed. It was a text from Rook, a local rapper I was doing some artwork for:

WHASSUP?

I typed back:

GOT HELD UP ON MY WAY

I had one more quick stop to make. I'm keepin' my hustle clean, but it's still a hustle. The tattoo shop don't pay all the bills. I gotta grind. Since so many people around town like my work, I started getting asked to do artwork for up-and-coming rappers like this DC kid named Rook, and small businesses in the hood like the one Juice owns. Most of my side work is word of mouth for now. Truth is, Rook is garbage on the mic, but that's not my concern. I'm about the cash.

Oh, don't get it twisted, he's involved in some shadyness, but I keep my dealings with him strictly about my artwork. He knows I'm no poser or punk, so he's never tested me. I ain't no snitch, and I'm not into judging you if that's how you get down. Things are just different for me now. I don't want any trouble or drama. I only want to make that paper, baby, doin' what I love, creating art. Word is bond! Like I said, Rook is wack lyrically, but he pays top dollar, cash money baby, when I do his CD covers on all his mixes and T-shirts.

All heads turned as I rolled up to Joe's Pool, a local old-school pool hall joint in the LeDroit Park neighborhood in northwest DC. Joe's is near Howard University, a prestigious historical black college right in the middle of the hood. I gotta say, I was feelin' myself in a lovely way pulling up in my sick new whip. Make no mistake, I might be a white dude, but I'm probably more comfortable in the hood anyway than I'd ever be in the burbs. Real peeps don't trip off the color of somebody's skin anyway.

"Whiteboy, you got that, playa!" My boy Wiz, who hangs out here regularly, threw up the peace sign, showin' me some love. I gave him a pound.

"She sweet, right?" I said, pointing toward my car before giving Wiz another pound and heading inside the pool hall.

But the one thing you *do* have to make sure of in the hood is to watch your back, front, and sides. Hustlas be straight doin' dirt. I don't ask questions. I get in and get out. Meeting at this spot was Rook's call.

"You got my masterpiece, Whiteboy!" Rook walked up to me and gave me a pound.

"And you know this!" I reached in my backpack and pulled out the color drawings for Rook's CD and one CD jewel case already made up.

"This shit is crazy, Whiteboy! You laced me once again! Yo, take a ride with me to the studio. My cash is there. Plus, I gotta meet this kid there who's gonna do a verse on one of my tracks. Come and check it out."

I didn't want to disrespect my man, but as bad as I needed my money, I felt too uncomfortable. I checked my watch. "Nah, Rook, I got a early day tomorrow. Why don't you meet me with the cash tomorrow?"

"C'mon, Whiteboy, not you? We used to run the streets all night."

"Not no more, Rook."

"C'mon. This is me, your boy Rook. Plus, you just got your

new ride outside. I just wanna play some of the new joints on the CD for you, and my cash to pay you is there. Follow me!" he said, patting me on the back.

How the hell did I get here? I kept sayin' to myself as I parked my car. I just didn't have a good feelin', but I tried not to look nervous. Rook's studio was plush, with flat screen TVs everywhere and a state-of-the-art system. He sparked up a blunt, passed it to me, and I took a deep puff. Rook proceeded to play track after track on his latest wack creation. I had to smoke damn near half the blunt to listen to it.

There was a knock. I jumped. When the door opened, I let out a silent sigh. A young kid about fifteen entered. He was clean-cut and walked through the room with confidence.

"Yo, whassup!" Rook gave the kid a pound. "Whiteboy, this is Young Tre. And the baddest young dude rappin' outta Anacostia. He mad smart too on that positive shit!" Rook added.

"You puttin' a lot on it, Rook, but I appreciate it," Young Tre modestly replied, then turned to me and gave me a pound.

"You about to spit?" I asked, nodding toward the recording booth.

"Most definitely." Young Tre headed into the booth and placed the headphones on his ears.

As I impatiently waited for Rook to set up the sound board with his engineer and play the last track, all I could think about was gettin' my money and gettin' outta there. When he put the track on, I found myself actually digging it.

"Yeah, yeah. A one, two, one, two." Young Tre closed his eyes and started feelin' the track. And then he spit like fire on the mic.

"You still talkin' 'bout cars, clothes, and dough. I'm talkin' 'bout whatchu know. Knowledge is my dough. Spend that paper wisely, yo. Like Wayne say, blind eyes could look at me and still see the truth. Young Tre's the name, and I got nothin' left to say!"

"Dope! That kid's flow is fi-yah!" I said, diggin' Young Tre's vibe even more. This kid had mad talent.

"Crazy, right? He's only fifteen and ill on the mic! You can have a copy of the CD first. Play it in your shop." He pulled it out of the stereo and handed it to me, along with a stack of cash. Fifteen hundred dollars! For doing the posters for his next show and the CD cover.

Just then we heard a loud ruckus and voices shouting from down the hallway. I quickly gathered my backpack and cash. Young Tre ran out of the booth.

"Roll out, Whiteboy! I know this ain't your get-down no more!" Rook motioned for me to leave and yelled for his homies Richie Rich and J Dub. They busted in through the side entrance. Then the studio door flew open, and all I saw were four hard-core heads bum-rush Rook and his boys. The leader was a smooth-looking Puerto Rican cat. He cut his eye at me. I knew I didn't have that bad feeling for no reason. I definitely didn't need this in my life right now.

My eyes darted around the room for the side door to escape. I grabbed Young Tre's arm, and we made a break for it, hopping in my car, and screeching off just as the sound of gunshots went off. The police sirens and flashing lights followed, zooming down the other end of the block. My heart was beating like crazy.

When we were far enough away, Tre motioned for me to drop him off at the Metro stop.

"This is cool right here," he said.

"Nah, young, I can take you all the way. You don't need to be out here this late," I said.

"Yo, I'm from Anacostia! This hood is *my* hood. Ain't nobody gonna bother me!" he said, getting out.

"I'm just lookin' out," I said, giving him a pound.

"I appreciate it, but if you wanna look out, why don't you hook me up on some of that dope artwork. I'm trying to get my own demo together."

"Yo, that ain't nothin' but a word! Let me just say that on the real, you're ill on the mic. I could definitely hook you up," I said, giving him my number.

"I'll be in touch. Whiteboy, right?" Tre said with a laugh.

"Hey, sometimes names just stick!" I said.

"I ain't trippin' about your name or the color of your skin. It's all in here," he said, pounding his chest. "I'm feelin' your work and that's whassup!" Tre said as we gave each other another pound before he ran off into the Metro tunnel. Damn, I guess he's right. Where he's from gunshots and cats wildin' out happens on the regular.

Twenty minutes later I pulled up in front of a small brick house. I let out a deep breath. As I made my way up the walkway, a tiny, old, plump Puerto Rican lady stepped out on the porch.

"Tommy! Is that chu?" she called out.

"Hey, Ms. H," I called back. It was Ms. Hernandez, my landlady. She always called me Tommy, my "government name," as the homies in the hood would say.

"I was almost going to sleep, but I had to see it. *Muy bonito!* That is one beautiful car!"

"Thanks, Ms. H. But you know you don't need to wait up for me. Plus, it's not that safe out here at night."

"No one's crazy enough to bother an old lady!" She laughed, turning to go back into the house. I headed down the side steps to the basement apartment that I rented from her.

I collapsed on my bed, heart still beating fast, and stared at the graffiti art I put on the ceiling. I grabbed the gold cross hanging from the chain on my necklace and quietly prayed to my grandma. *Dear Grandma, I got a new start here in DC. I'm not going to blow it. I promise.* I was just happy to have gotten out of Rook's studio without crazy drama. I hit the lights. The last thing I needed was to catch a case.

CHAPTER FIVE

BLUE

I've never been afraid
Fresh and I'm gettin' paid . . .
—Common featuring Pharrell, "Universal Mind Control"

Homecoming night had arrived and the jam-packed SSH gymnasium was proof that the name Blue Reynolds was as reliable as the postal service—I had delivered. Collin and I were chillin' onstage, sitting on top of one of the deejay's giant speakers while Whiteboy leaned against it. We were all bobbing our heads to the music, taking in the room's energy. A flurry of waves, thumbs-ups, and peace signs from the crowd were being thrown in my direction. Posters with my face covered the gym walls. I felt like royalty.

"Yo, check out that girl in the front row," I said, pointing to a honey-skinned beauty who was barely dancing. "She's amazing. Who is she?" Out of all the girls here, she stood out for some reason.

I zeroed in on her, and everything else in the room stopped.

"Look at her smile, and, damn, she's got a body like Rihanna's!"

"She's probably stuck up. C'mon, playboy, this song is bangin' and she's doin' that wack two-step. Yo, you stick with the snobby one. I'm gonna go scoop me a hot one!" Whiteboy said, dashing off to the dance floor.

"I don't know her. I've never seen her at SSH before," Collin said, taking note.

"Well, we *should* know her and every other bad babe up in here. The honeys came out of the woodwork for this joint. I swear, if this is what fame brings, I want in. I'm diggin' this movement. I've definitely caught the entertainment business bug," I proclaimed.

"You're joking, right?" Collin chuckled.

"Am I laughing? Yo, I've decided I want in. I could start promoting my own parties, but on some new level, shiznit!" Collin gave me a crazy look.

"Dude, please don't tell me this is going to your head. It's *just* a party. Keep it in perspective," Collin said with skepticism.

"Think I'm playin'? We could be stackin' dollars." I winked.

"*We!* Where did the plurals come from? Dude, I got college, law school, a career to think about!" Collin said, shaking his head furiously.

"Collin, we got plenty of time to think about college. You could be my partner in this. You know how to put ideas in motion, man. Plus, we're younger and hotter than anybody out here doin' parties in Silver Spring for sure. Hell, DC for that matter. This is just a starting place. Just like cats like Russell Simmons passed the baton to guys like Diddy. Diddy became a household name. Diddy unlocked the door, and I'm gonna kick it in! It's time for somebody else to reign," I said, transfixed by the flashing lights in the room. "I've got it! What do you think about the name Blue Up Productions?" I announced as if I was actually seeing it in big lights. "I'm tryin' to make moves with the likes of people like that guy Rico Tate. We could be throwing parties at his clubs!"

"Slow down, Blue," Collin said, raising his hands in a halt gesture. "These things have to be thought out."

"What's there to think out?" I asked.

"Okay, for one, you can't expect somebody like Rico Tate to just hand over one of his venues. We don't have a track record!"

"Okay, so forget Rico. I'll go to someone else. My point is that you take this," I said referring to the action in the room. "And you flip it into having a record company or something," I said enthusiastically.

"Maybe, but that's passé. What you want is distribution and muscle on the Internet. We've got to own what we do," Collin added.

"Exactly! We could go global. Hold up, you said 'we.' So does that mean you're in?" I eyed him hard. He knew I meant business, and there was no turning back. There was a long silent pause. "Collin, it's all about us making our own way. I don't want to live my life for my father. Maybe I'll be a lawyer. Then again, maybe I won't. What about you?"

"I *do* want to be a lawyer, but I agree with you. I definitely want to make my *own* way. I want it on my own terms." Collin stood up and started pacing back and forth. "I could grab hold of my future and not have to have it handed to me on some golden platter for my dad to hang it over my head for the rest of my life!"

"We could make so much money you'd have enough to pay your own way through law school!" I said, giving him a pound. Suddenly we heard a building chant from the crowd. "Blue! Blue! Blue! Blue!"

"Dude, they're calling for you out there," he said as we both looked over the crowd.

"This is serious power. Seriously, I need to get at that guy Rico Tate immediately!" I said, jumping off the speaker. "It's time to kick this party into overdrive!"

I dashed toward center stage and started waving my hands in the air back and forth, and the crowd followed my direction. "Ho, hay, ho, hay!" I chanted, starting a call-and-response. "When I say 'Get it,' you say 'Money!' Get it!"

"Money!" the crowd shouted back.

I repeated it a few more times before signaling to the deejay. "DJ Nice, drop that Lil Wayne nice and low! First off, respect and love to all! And before I go any further I wanna give a special shout-out to the honey right here in the front row! What's up, mami? You are gorgeous!" I pointed and waved to the mystery girl I had my eye on earlier and winked. All the girls started screaming.

Unfortunately, I guess she didn't find my shout-out very amusing. She curled up her lips, shook her head, gave me the hand, and pushed her way to the back of the crowd. Damn! Where did she go? I scanned the room to no avail. "Okay, okay, back to the business at hand. Let's bring out our newly crowned king and queen!" As the king and queen and their court gathered on the stage, my eyes kept searching for my mystery girl. No luck.

I rejoined Collin, who was now standing with Whiteboy.

"So, C says you're gonna be a businessman!" Whiteboy teased. "Oh, snap. You're really tryin' to make moves like ya boy Rico Tate.

"That's what I'm talkin' about. By the way, how about a shot to be Blue Up's creative go-to guy? You can be in charge of creating our logo, and all the flyers and club promotional materials," I said, extending my hand.

"Word up! Let's get it poppin'!" Whiteboy said.

"I want you to do some of those Coming Soon posters and flyers. We gotta blow up Blue Up Productions! I think this is our time, for real!"

"First thing I gotta do is find us the right venue. Not too big, but definitely where we could get a good starting crowd." Now the wheels were churning in Collin's brain too.

"I wanna do a monthly joint, then maybe when things start building up, move to bimonthly," I said.

"Unfortunately, we're going to need some start-up cash flow," Collin reminded.

"Yo, y'all are my boys and I ain't got much after getting my new ride, but I got five hundred if you need it," Whiteboy said.

"Thanks, man. Everything will help. You know I'll get it back to you as soon as I can," I said, putting my fist out. "We could use it to get the promotional hype going. I want to put up those posters and flyers around school, especially as kids enter the Cyber Café."

"Blue, my only fear is that we got nothing right now. Why not wait until we book a venue?" Collin asked skeptically.

"Look, the entertainment game is ninety percent smoke and mirrors. It's okay that we don't even have our first party yet. It's about generating the energy, setting the tone for what's coming. I'm talking an all-out assault on Facebook and every social networking site we can think of. I want us passing out business cards to everyone we meet. Money attracts money. Hype attracts hype. We make our plans while we put our plan in action. We've gotta blow up Blue Up Productions! And we need a logo ASAP too! We want Blue Up to be the first name in teen entertainment."

"Yo, that's whassup! You got it, baby! The logo will take time. I want it to be right, but I can definitely get some cool graphics going for the Net and all the other stuff you need for print." Whiteboy stuck his fist out, next to mine. "The world is yours, baby!" he proclaimed.

"I'm down even though I think this is, with all due respect, ass backward, but to hell with it. Let's make it happen!" Collin added his fist to the circle and we sealed our fate.

I guess sometimes you have to throw caution to the wind and go for what you know in your heart. I know there are going to be haters trying to bring us down, but you have to put the blinders on and just come hard. When it's your shot, you gotta take it!

INTRODUCING

JADE TAYLOR

the Believer

CHAPTER SIX

JADE

I'm sick and tired of the loose rap
—Aaliyah, "Loose Rap"

"So what's up, chickie!" my girl Mamie screeched midbite into her double cheeseburger, during our girlfriend chow-down in the food court at the City Place Mall, in downtown Silver Spring.

"Well, I think I need to get a job," I said, stuffing another french fry into my mouth.

"What! You want to join the land of the working?" Mamie teased. I playfully swatted her.

"I'm desperate for the money." I took a frustrated bite of my burger. "Things are really getting tight around our house. Plus, I have to start thinking about college. Two years isn't that far away. Even with every scholarship known to man, it's gonna take *M-O-N-E-Y*. Pass the ketchup, please." I reached for my milk shake. Mamie looked at me like I had two heads.

"You really want a job? Humph! Girl, you're Miss Bookworm. How are you gonna maintain that four-point with a job? Plus, you ain't hardly used to hard labor like me!"

"Nothing's going to keep me from being a doctor! I'll dig ditches, whatever! For real, I'm not some scared little girl. My mom is all I have, and I owe it to her. It's time for me to pull my weight at home. Besides, how hard can waiting tables be?"

"Hello! Feisty, aren't we? I wasn't up for all this serious talk. Can we at least just get through the rest of junior year first? I've never heard you sound like this before."

"Whatever, are you going to help me or what?" I asked, looking her squarely in the eyes.

"You're my girl. Of course. I can definitely get my boss to hook you up on a part-time gig. I think we've got an opening for another waitress on my evening shift. Girl, we could kick it! Busboys and Poets is such a chill spot, you could even get some of your studying done between customer flow!" Mamie chomped as she poured a mound of ketchup on a small side plate to dunk her fries.

"Cool. Now all I have to do is convince my mom that I can work *and* go to school." I let out a sigh.

"Jade, you look so worried. Are you being totally straight with me about what's going on in your life?"

"Look, there's a lot going on, but I don't want to really deal with it today. Just look out for me. Things are complicated, but I can handle it."

"Is it your mom's health again?"

"No, no, she's great, really great. I just need to help out, you know?" I said, uneasily shifting in my seat. Mamie was eyeballing me. "I'm fine, really. I just need a job!" I said.

"Okay. I'll leave it alone," she said, throwing her hands up in a surrendering gesture. "But know I'm here for you," she said, touching my hand. I could feel myself welling up with tears. The last thing I wanted to do was cry. "We're gonna get you that job. In the meantime, here. It ain't much, but I've been saving. This is for you. Put it in the future college fund!" Mamie handed me two twenties and a ten.

"I can't take your money, Mae," I said, fighting back the tears to no avail, as I looked down at the fifty dollars in my hand. I wiped my eyes.

"Aw, damn, you know I'm not into that sensitive stuff. Cut it out!" We both laughed. "I didn't loan you that money. I gave it to you. Considering I'm not shooting for the honor roll or college, it would be a shame for my graduation and college fund to go to waste. And besides, one day, after you finish all that school stuff and become a rich doctor, and I'm the hottest multiplatinum Grammy-winning female music producer in the business, we'll sit around on your yacht wearing fabulous gear, rockin' our ice, laughing about the days when we were broke!"

We both burst into laughter, before gobbling down the rest

of our fast-food feast. When we finished, I started clearing the table.

"I'm working from four to eight today at the café, and then I'm going to that club in Adams Morgan. I've been beggin' the promoter to put me on the turntables and give me a night. He at least lets me get five or ten minutes here and there. I gotta keep hustlin'," Mamie said, pulling out her compact and applying fresh lip gloss. Girlfriend's makeup against her flaw-less cocoa skin always had to be just right. She ran her fingers through her fresh-from-the-salon tresses. "So whassup? You rollin' with me tonight?" she said, carefully brushing mascara onto her eyelashes.

"Mae, c'mon. It's a school night. I love you, but no. I got to stay focused on the books, try to get ahead, especially since I'm going to hopefully get a job. Clubbin' is not one of my subjects," I said.

"I know. I still thought I'd ask. But when I finally book one of those really hot clubs to spin at, or a major gig, I don't care what day of the week it is. You'd betta be there front and center!"

"You know I will." I dumped the trash in a nearby container.

"Damn, you're pretty good at that. I see part-time waitress in your future!" she said, wrapping her colorful scarf around her head like a turban, pretending to be a fortune-teller.

"The only thing is that Busboys and Poets is so far from my

house. I live in Pettworth, and Fourteenth and V Streets are in midtown. That's at least twenty minutes away in a car. A car I don't have. Taking the Metro at night—oh, no. My mom will never go for that."

"Yeah, well, hello. Your girl does have a car, when it works. We'll get on the same shifts, and when you work nights, I'll drive you home or we'll catch the Metro together. C'mon. I've got forty minutes before I have to get ready for work. Let's shop!" Mamie, in true dramatic form, put on her oversize sunglasses and was now wrapping her scarf around her neck like some rich diva.

"Uh, excuse me. With what money? I just had to take a handout from you," I said, with my hands on my hips.

"It's called window-shopping, girlie!" Mamie grabbed my arm and dragged me off to Urban Outfitters.

As soon as we walked into the store, Mamie, aka Miss Fashionista, went straight for the back display. "Oh, my God. I would look crazy in that spinning at the club!" she said, pointing to a micromini jean skirt and cowboy boots. She hurriedly slipped the boots on.

"Girlie, you'd definitely look fabulous deejaying in those!" I said.

"Miss, she'll try a pair on in eight and a half," she called out to the salesperson. There was never a dull moment with Mamie. Before I could say no, I was slipping on a pair of boots. Mamie and I were acting crazy like we had money to spend.

"Jade, those are hot!" Mamie admired.

"You think so, Mae? I think they look better on you," I said, looking in the full-length mirror.

"I think they look great on both of you!" A guy's voice startled us from behind. I turned around quickly to see who it was coming from. The voice belonged to the sweetest pair of brown eyes, sporting a pair of aviators, dressed in preppy-conservative flavor.

"Can we help you?" Mamie said in a flirtatious tone, giving the cute stranger the once-over.

"I'm Collin Andrews," he said, holding out his hand.

"And I'm Mamie." Mamie put one hand on her hip and reciprocated the gesture, extending her other perfectly manicured hand. My girl was *such* a flirt.

"Errum." I inconspicuously cleared my throat. Mamie was too busy blushing.

"My bad. This is my girl Jade," Mamie said.

"Sorry for the rudeness," Collin said with an embarrassed look. "Here. I wanted to give you ladies some information about a new site introducing you to Silver Spring's finest in nightlife. Coming very soon to a club near you. You all go to school around here?" Collin handed us a colorful postcard with a picture of a cute guy's face on it.

"Yeah, we go to Silver Spring High," Mamie said as I checked out the party postcard.

"Wait, I think I saw you at the homecoming dance. Jade, right?" He eyed me curiously.

"Probably not. I was only there for a bit. Anyway, it's a big school. I'm in honors classes mostly, and I *don't* socialize much," I said.

"And I don't get to school much," Mamie said, and snickered, eyeing the postcard. "Hey, this is that guy Blue Reynolds, huh? I saw his posters everywhere during homecoming."

"Well, I'm Blue Reynolds's partner in Blue Up."

"Oh, snap. Partner? I heard that. Yeah, yeah, Blue Up Productions, thas whassup! Facebook has been on fire about you guys and how you turned out the blackout party *and* homecoming." She nodded. "I couldn't make it to either. I was working both nights," Mamie said, looking at the card again.

"You all should join our networking site," Collin encouraged.

"Oh, I don't waste my time with that stuff. Sorry," I added, rolling my eyes.

"It's cool. I do. I'm on Facebook. In fact, if you're looking for the hottest female deejay on the ones and twos in the Silver Spring–DC area, I might be able to hook you up with her," Mamie said, giving two snaps in the air.

"And who would that be?" another curious voice asked from across the room.

"That would be me!" Mamie turned around and said confidently. I followed her lead, and we both looked up and down at the new stranger, who was chomping on a toothpick.

"Sup, C!" He approached coolly, giving Collin a pound. Oh,

my God. It was the cute guy on the postcard who was onstage at the dance. "Ladies?"

"Mamie and Jade, this is Blue Reynolds," Collin said. "Coincidentally, they attend SSH. You might remember *Jade* from the homecoming dance," Collin hinted.

"Front row, right?" He nodded at me. I suddenly felt the weight of this handsome new stranger's eyes all over me like a cheap knockoff outfit.

"He was the obnoxious jerk who shouted me out on the mic," I whispered to Mamie. Honestly, I was both flattered and uncomfortable. I tried to play it off by looking away. This Blue was about five-ten, lean but muscular, and I'm not gonna lie, totally *H-O-T*. He had almost a boyish charm. And, oh, my God! His big brown eyes and million-dollar Colgate smile almost had a girl hypnotized.

"I hear your game is tight on the mic." Mamie giggled. "Mine is too. Professionally, I'm known as Ill Mama," she said excitedly.

"She's the sickest deejay around," I added, shaking off my obvious instant crush.

"Where do you spin?" Collin asked.

"Um, I do a, um, li'l somethin' somethin' at the Spot in Adams Morgan. I turn it out up in there." I shot Mamie a hard look. She was totally lying.

"That's cool. I'd love to check you out." Collin nodded.

"Yo, Jade, sorry if I embarrassed you at the party. I just

thought you were gorgeous and I had to holla at you," Blue butted in. His words dripped with charm.

"Well, some girls might find that appealing, but I don't," I said.

"It doesn't matter now. All that matters is that it's Blue Up's lucky day. Bam!" Mamie passed one of her own promo cards to both Collin and Blue. "You can check me and my beats out on Facebook. By the way, if you have any parties coming up and you want them to really be fly, Mr. Blue Reynolds, you'll hire me to deejay."

"I'll wait for my boy to give me the full report when he checks you out," Blue said cockily, removing the toothpick from his mouth.

"Whatever, dude," Mamie said, giving Blue the hand.

"Mamie, let me get your info," Collin said, pulling her over to the side.

"Can I check you out too, Jade?" Blue eyed me. Okay, he just blew it with that lame line.

"Is that how you meet girls?" I said, rolling my eyes.

"Only the beautiful ones. So can I call you?" he asked.

"No, I don't think so," I said, shaking my head.

"You got a man?"

"What?"

"You married?"

"Of course not!" I smiled, somewhat amused by his crazy line of questioning.

"So, where can I find you at school?" Before I could answer, he did the ultimate jerk move and started texting someone in the middle of our conversation! How disrespectful. No, he was not tryin' to play me out!

"Excuse me? How rude! You want to know where to find me, figure it out!" I said putting my hands on my hips.

"Huh? What did I do?" he asked, as if he had done nothing wrong.

"We were in the middle of talking, and that whole texting move was wack. Whatever! C'mon, Mae," I mumbled, rolling my eyes. Yuck. I was totally turned off by his nonchalant attitude. I couldn't believe the nerve of this guy. On second thought, he wasn't that hot. I grabbed Mamie's arm and pulled her away from her one-on-one with Collin.

"Hey, we gotta bounce, but don't sleep on the Ill Mama, Collin!" Mamie called out as I dragged her away.

"Let's go before you make up anything else about your so-called *set* at the Spot!" I said, quickly putting my sneakers back on, and motioning for Mamie to do the same. "Besides, Blue was a total jerk!" I said, pulling Mamie out of the store.

"Ouch! He may be a jerk, but girlie, that was my shot!" Mamie huffed.

"He's arrogant. Forget him. You don't need people like that. You're gonna make it because you've got *it*! You are much too talented and fly to waste your time. People like that guy make me sick. You don't have to beg anybody for anything!"

"I feel you." I could tell Mamie was a little disappointed.

"I wouldn't be your BFF if I didn't keep it real with you. Just know he's not the only game in town!"

"You're right. It ain't like he's Diddy or somebody!" Mamie was getting amped up again.

"Hello! Plus, those guys are still in high school like us. I would strongly question their credibility. Screw them!" I pumped her up again.

"Screw them!" Mamie checked the clock on her cell phone. "Oh, snap. I gotta jet for work. Oh, and I'm all over that job for you. Keep your head up, mami! Muah!" Mamie gave me an air kiss, grabbed her oversize faux designer tote, and bounced off.

"I'll call you later!" I laughed to myself at how absolutely adorable and funny my girl is. I headed off in the opposite direction. I swear, when it feels like the whole world is sitting on your shoulders, there's nothing like your BFF having your back.

BLUE UP
PRODUCTIONS
ENTERTAINMENT

DC's FINEST

COMING SOON!
IN 2009

CHAPTER SEVEN

BLUE

**Let me show you what it is right now
Let me . . . step up and handle my biz right now
—Busta Rhymes, "What It Is"**

A few days later Collin and I stood in front of the Cyber Café's bulletin board admiring Whiteboy's artistic masterpiece.

"So what do you think?" he asked.

"It's dope!" I said, giving him a major pound.

"Oh, hey, I want you to meet the guys I've been talking about." Collin motioned for two freshmen-looking dudes who were huddled a few feet away to join us. "Blue, this is Jullian and Taylor. Blue Up's new street team!"

"Whassup, Blue," Jullian said, shaking my hand. He was well-dressed and had that pretty-boy look.

"Glad to be down," Taylor said. He was more the athletic type with dreads.

It was all good. Collin had the Blue Up street team strategically place our BLUE UP PRODUCTIONS: COMING SOON posters in all the high-visibility areas at SSH.

"Okay, guys, hit me later after all the signs are out at the other high schools!" Collin instructed. Jullian and Taylor raced off.

"I like those cats!" I said.

"Dude, I hired those freshmen, to work for free of course, to do the leg- and word-of-mouth work. Their job is to run around town hitting the three other Silver Spring high schools with our promo flyers and postcards on an ongoing basis. I told them that they'll get in free and VIP status at all Blue Up events. Sweet, right!"

"Brilliant!" I gave him a high five.

"I'll catch you later. I'm headed to the library," Collin said before jetting in the opposite direction.

Silver Spring was just minutes from the DC city limits, but I agreed with Collin that we needed to master our part of town first before moving our operation into DC proper. Our marketing assault on the Net was in effect too. For right now all the wording was generic and on a TBA basis, but it was part of the plan. We were succeeding in spreading the word that Blue Up was about to take over the party game. The only drag to what felt like an incredible day was that Mr. Richardson had succeeded in setting up that appointment with my college counselor.

I opened the door to the college counseling office and grabbed a vacant seat outside Mr. Jones's office.

"Hey, Blue." A short and perky blonde waved. A cute brown-skinned cheerleader type with a ponytail met up with her, and as they headed out the door, she turned and waved. "Hi, Blue. We loved you at homecoming. Can't wait for those parties!"

"Whassup, ladies. Thanks for the love." I casually waved back. They ran out giggling. I'm not trying to come off with some inflated ego, but I did get a kick out of the way those girls reacted. It's like my stock had already gone up.

"Blue, Mr. Jones will see you now," Ms. Hightower, the counseling office secretary, said in a nasally voice. My meeting was supposed to be at three o'clock. I had been waiting for fifteen minutes. I just wanted to get this over with. She motioned for me to follow her. When I finally sat down in Mr. Jones's office my phone started buzzing almost immediately. He shot me a look. I chuckled nervously, offering a half smile. It was an urgent message from Whiteboy:

YO RICO TATE COMING TO SHOP
@4 GET YO ASS HERE
C ON IS WAY . . . GTB FO LIFE—WB

Oh, hell yeah! "GTB" in our world meant "get that bread." In other words, get that money! Rico Tate was just the guy I needed to get at. Today was not the day to talk about college. Besides, I had a major dilemma now. I had to be at Whiteboy's shop, Cutz and Tatz, at four sharp. It was three fifteen—correction, three seventeen—and I'd be damned if I missed my chance to talk to Rico Tate.

Ten minutes later, Mr. Jones was still reading my college essay and sifting through papers in a folder labeled BLUE REYNOLDS. Can you believe it? I shifted in my seat numerous times and impatiently tapped my foot. I thought, *How can I let Mr. Jones know that if I don't leave now, I'm going to miss getting hooked up?*

"Mr. Reynolds," he said in a serious tone. "I've been your adviser for the past three years, and I know your parents personally. We attended Howard University together, but as I read and reread your college essay and your papers that Mr. Richardson forwarded to me, it just doesn't seem like you put one hundred percent into things. I know how important Howard is to your father."

"Quite frankly, Mr. Jones, Howard is a fine institution, but college is the last thing on my list of priorities right now. And being a lawyer is even farther down my list. I'm just not sure at this time."

"Have you talked about this with your father?" he asked.

"I can't. You don't understand. He would bug out. I mean, be very *disappointed*. It's not that I don't want to go to college *one* day, but I've got some big ideas. And I'm on the verge of making one of them pop off. I mean, *happen*." I nervously looked down at my buzzing phone. It was Collin this time blowin' up my Sidekick.

DUDE JUST ROLLED UP.
WHERE U AT? GTB GTB GTB

"Mr. Jones, I'm supposed to meet *the* Rico Tate right now! This is the break I need." By now I was sweating bullets.

"Mr. Reynolds," Mr. Jones said, and let out an exhausted sigh. "Clearly I don't have a chance competing with Mr. Rico Tate, whoever that is, for your attention. Unfortunately, I don't think you fully understand the importance of getting that college degree. Now, whether or not you become a lawyer is not my call, but I think you need to understand the repercussions, Mr. Reynolds, of not having a college degree. So, let's put a pin in this, and I think you and your parents should come in and talk about things. . . ." Before he could finish, I was gone like the wind.

I was sitting at the red light a block away from the shop, but I could see the sign for Cutz and Tatz ahead. The light turned green and I sped off. My tires came to a screeching halt behind a tinted-out Maybach. Collin and Whiteboy were standing out front already. I jumped out of my mom's car, leaving it running, and raced up to Rico's driver, who was just closing the passenger door, where Rico was sitting.

"Excuse me. I need to talk to Mr. Tate right away!" I pleaded. The gargantuan-size man who looked like a WWF reject held his hands out, halting me.

"Don't get hurt, young playa!" he threatened, reaching into his jacket. My boys Collin and Whiteboy, who were clearly as insane as I was at this point, ran to cover my back in case this fool decided to break every bone in my body.

"Yo, whassup, Snake. You got a problem? All that ain't necessary," Whiteboy said, standing up to him.

"C'mon, Blue, this isn't worth it." Collin tried to pull me away.

"I'm cool. I'm cool," I said. "Look, you don't understand. No disrespect, but I'm a party promoter and I want to talk to Mr. Tate about doing business with him." I was desperate at this point. Just then the passenger door opened and out stepped Rico Tate.

"Back up, Snake," Mr. Tate ordered his bodyguard. "Listen, I don't know who you are, but I suggest you get out the way and get back in your car. I'm trying to save your mama some tears." He chuckled.

"But please, Mr. Tate. Just hear me out!" I was begging mercilessly.

"This is actually quite amusing. Who are you and what do you want?"

"Well, sir, um, my name is Blue Reynolds and I want to team up with you in the teen nightlife world," I nervously stumbled.

"You want to *team up* with me?" He started laughing hysterically. "Well, Blake—"

"Blue," I said, cutting him off.

"Blake, Blue, whatever the fuck your name is, I don't know who you are or what you've done. I didn't make my millions on teen parties. Do you have a track record? Do you have an artist I might be interested in?" I was dumbfounded. "I'm in the major leagues, son. You got nothing. Time is money, and as far as I'm concerned, this little episode is over. Don't ever waste my time again. Build your rep and come correct. Let's go, Snake." He laughed again.

"Oh, and a word to the wise: Make this the first and last time you ever roll up on me. People get hurt like that." He returned to his car and winked, disappearing behind the tinted windows. His bodyguard backed away, and within seconds me, Collin, and Whiteboy were sucking on the exhaust fumes from Rico Tate's car.

"I played myself!" I shouted in frustration.

"Dude, what you just did took a lot of balls," Collin said, patting me on the shoulder.

"It's fools like that that make it hard for me not to pull my heater out and smoke they asses," Whiteboy said, with narrowed eyes.

"No, I gotta get a plan. This whole thing with Rico wouldn't have been ruined if Mr. Jones had let me out of that meeting on time."

"Blue, you've gotta let it go. It won't be the last time with Rico," Collin replied. "I'm a believer that timing is everything, and maybe it just wasn't time for you to hook up with him. Maybe we need more *time* to come at him."

"Collin, tell me I didn't hear you correctly. You're supposed to be my partner and have my back. You know, back my play, pass the rock so I can take it to the hole. Whassup?"

"Blue, I'm just saying that you want the proper introduction. You don't wanna be sweatin' this guy Rico. I don't care how powerful he is. I mean, coming down here to the shop was a long shot anyway," Collin stressed.

"Wait! I'm not gonna make it waiting for somebody to give me a shot. I gotta take it. I thought you were down. Nobody told Diddy to wait!" I shouted. There was a tense moment of silence.

"Both of y'all need to chill and just talk this thing out." Whiteboy stepped in as the voice of reason.

"Rico Tate is right. We got nothing, nothing but a bunch of talk. Maybe what he said about having some talent that's hot is the key to getting in with him. I just need time to think."

"I'll start thinkin' too." Collin took a deep breath. "Maybe I should check out the girl we met, Mamie," Collin said.

"You mean the deejay chick from the mall?" I asked, shooting an incredulous look. "You think she's hot, don't you?"

"Whatever, dude. She's definitely hot, but that's not why I suggested her. I think we have nothing to lose," Collin added.

"Yo, B, he does have a point," Whiteboy said, giving Collin a nod.

"Maybe. I don't know." I could feel the frustration swelling in my gut again. Hearing DJ Ill Mama's name wasn't the golden goose I was looking for. "I just know it's time to get on the grind and find some talent!" I said, slamming my fists on the hood of my mom's car. I'd really blown it with Rico Tate, but I couldn't let that defeat me. I was determined to go back with my game tighter and hit him on a whole other level.

INTRODUCING

MAMIE

the Survivor

FRAZIER

Superstar Deejay

I'm not the girl that you knew before
I can't believe you didn't know I'm grown
—Tiffany Evans, "I'm Grown"

"Hey, Mamie, it looks like you've got a new boyfriend," Rene, the club hostess, whispered in my ear as she pointed toward the bar. "That guy over there is looking for you." Collin was leaning against the bar sipping on a Red Bull with his back to me.

"Guess who?" I said, swooping in on him and covering his eyes with my hands.

"Hey!" Collin jumped with surprise. I pulled my hands away so he could see it was me. "You look great. I was taking a chance coming down. I wasn't sure if you were spinning or not, but I remembered you said you had a set here, and I was nearby," Collin said.

"Well, I'm glad you came down. But I gotta be honest, I don't have an *official* set," I said, using air quotes. "The owner just slides me in when the regular deejay goes on breaks, and that's usually for no more than five or ten minutes. But, hey, it's an opportunity. It's cool that you decided you were ready to roll with tha flava, though. You came at the right time too. I go up in about five minutes."

"Cool. I'll hang around and check you out," Collin said, giving me a thumbs-up.

"Relax!" I winked, and then quickly made my way to the deejay booth.

I knew I didn't have much time, but I had to impress the hell out of Collin. I placed my headphones over my ears and pulled the mic toward me. "What's up, party people. I'm DJ Ill Mama, the baddest femme fatale behind the wheels of steel in a pair of stilettos, and it's goin' down here at the Spot and I'm about to take you on what I like to call the grown and sexy ride. So get yo asses up and let's get this!"

I dropped the needle on that vintage Vanity 6, "Nasty Girl." My body swayed back and forth as the music carried me into a state of euphoria. Then I scratched in some of that A Tribe Called Quest, "Bonita Applebaum." I looked up and caught Collin's eye. He was diggin' that old-school love I was throwing from the crate.

I know a lot of deejays nowadays strictly spin on their laptops and use mini discs, and I have some of that same equipment. But when I'm behind two turntables with that microphone in my hand, it's clear that the new-school methods just don't have that heart and soul. Nothing compares to the feeling I get from that album wax under my fingertips.

After I finished my mini set, I rejoined Collin at the bar.

"So what do you think?" I asked.

"I think you're incredible. Why aren't you spinning regularly here, or anyplace else for that matter?" he asked, draining his Red Bull.

"Yo, it's hard out here for a sista. I've been tryin', but fools won't give me any love. Believe it or not, it's still very sexist on the deejay scene. That's why hooking up with you and your man would be crazy! I'm working on a mix CD, but I'll get it to you soon."

"Cool. We're really still organizing some things, so let's keep in touch," he said, checking his watch. "I gotta jet. Now that I know you, I'll start looking for you at school, too," he said as we walked toward the door.

"Yeah, school." I chuckled. "I told you I don't really dig school, so don't bank on it. I've been on my own schedule lately, but hit me up on Facebook or shoot me a text, or most of the time you can catch me here." I gave him a hug. Although Collin didn't make any promises, I was hopeful, because he had seen my skills in person.

"Mamie? Mamie? Mamie, get up! You're going to be late for school, and I need to talk to you before I go to work!" My aunt Deb was standing at my bedroom door sweatin' me again. "Mamie, I know you hear me! Get up now! I need to talk to you!"

"Urgh!" I let out a big sigh, then rolled over, sat up, and looked at the clock. It was six thirty a.m. Was she out of her mind? "What?" I whined. "I totally haven't had any sleep, Aunt Deb. You know I was up late working on my music."

"Get up, wash your face, and meet me in the kitchen! Three minutes!" When Aunt Deb raised her voice, she meant business. I just wasn't up for any lectures. I worked at the café before going to do that short set at the Spot. I should've known Aunt Deb was gonna trip about me coming in so late.

I rinsed my face with cold water and then did a quick swish of mouthwash, slipped on a pair of sweats, and made it into the kitchen in record time.

"I said three minutes. That was five. Sit down!" Aunt Deb scolded, taking a sip of coffee. My aunt was my father's baby sister, unmarried and no kids. She could be tough. Maybe that was why she didn't have a man. After my stepmother kicked me out three years ago, and my father didn't stand up for me, I moved in with her.

"Mamie, when I opened my home to you, I said we'd get along as long as you followed my rules. Rule number one was going to school and doing your best. Rule number two was keeping up with your chores. And rule number three was no boys up in my house."

"And what's the beef," I said, pouring myself a glass of orange juice and taking a sip.

"Do you think I'm stupid? This came from the school, and I found it in the trash. It's a notice about your grades," she said, slamming a crumpled piece of paper on the table.

"Whatever," I said, sucking my teeth.

"No! Not whatever. What the hell is going on! I work too hard to keep a decent roof over our heads. I've made a lot of sacrifices because you needed a stable environment to live in. I agreed to you working and even hanging in the clubs, because you said this music thing was your passion, but you're abusing my generosity. You haven't been going to classes. What the hell do you think I'm running here!"

"I just had some things that came up. I'll start going to class. Cool?"

"Everything is not cool all the damn time! Mamie, you're not stupid, but you're acting like you are right now. Maybe you think life is a joke, but I'm here to tell you it's not. You're going to see how unfunny life really is when you have to start paying rent and bills. And I'm sorry, princess, but spinning some records ain't gonna mean crap on a résumé. You can't get anywhere without a high school diploma, and what about college?"

"Maybe college isn't for me. Maybe school period isn't for me! I'm good at making my music, and I'm sorry that doesn't meet your approval." I stood up and started out of the kitchen.

"Don't you dare walk out this room!"

"I've gotta get ready for school," I said.

"You've been warned, young lady. And as far as that smart-ass mouth of yours, remember, you've got one more year of high school, and after that, fine, you're on your own. Until then you'd better damn well adhere to my rules!"

"And if I don't?"

"Then you'd better find somewhere else to live."

We were at a standoff, face-to-face. I knew Aunt Deb meant business, but maybe it was time I made some decisions of my own.

"Don't take my words lightly, Mamie." Aunt Deb rolled her eyes, grabbed her purse and keys, and stormed out of the house. I leaned up against the wall and let out a big sigh, and then stomped off to my bedroom.

I placed my headphones over my ears and dropped the needle on the wax, the rock and roll classic "Under Pressure" by Queen and David Bowie. Then I mixed in some classic hip-hop and R & B with Mary J Blige's "No More Drama." That's exactly what I needed in my life right now—no more drama! All I needed was two turntables and a mic in my hand to feel better.

I leaned back on my bed, hoping the music would take me to another space and time, but my thoughts were racing. Have you ever felt like everywhere you went no one wanted you? Or that you just didn't belong? That's how I've felt most of my life. Maybe that's why I don't trust anybody outside of my best friend, Jade. Like Beyoncé says, I can only depend on me, myself, and I. I surely couldn't depend on Aunt Deb anymore, as evidenced by that morning.

Out of frustration I scratched the needle across the record, ripped off my headphones, and pounded my fist into the pillow. I paced the floor for a few minutes, the nervous energy jumping all over my body. I wiped my tears, then went to my crate of records and pulled out the twelve-inch vinyls of Unk's "Walk It Out" and Nelly's "Grillz." I placed the albums on the turntables and dropped the needles onto the records, simultaneously, grabbing my headphones and putting them back on. When the beat dropped, I let out a deep breath, mixing the two songs with intense fury. I was in my element. Music is my savior!

CHAPTER NINE

Catch da holy ghost at my shows like ya grandma at church
—Ludacris, "Undisputed"

I woke up at the crack of dawn this morning, and I was out in my driveway shooting hoops for an hour. All I kept thinking about was how I missed my shot with Rico. Maybe it took a couple of days for it to finally sink in just how bad he dissed me? I was still at ground zero—no talent to showcase or angle to go back to him with. Man, I thought getting some exercise would take my mind off things, but it wasn't working. I stood at the imaginary free-throw line, dribbled, then shot. *Swish!* Nothing but net.

"Blue?" My dad called out. "Are you okay?"

"Yeah, Dad, I'm cool," I replied flatly, shooting the ball

again, this time missing. I jogged over to the bottom of the front steps, where the ball rolled to a stop.

"Son, I don't know what's going on with you, but something is. I'm here for you," he said, standing in the doorway. "Is it school?"

"No."

"Is it a girl?"

"No," I found myself laughing a bit. "I don't have problems in that area."

"Well, Mr. Smooth," my dad joked, "when you're ready to talk about it, I'm all ears. Maybe in the meantime you should come in and shower and get ready for church.

"Yes, sir," I cracked, picking up my ball and darting up the front steps two at a time.

"Son," he said, stopping me before we went back inside the house. "I know sometimes church isn't the coolest thing to do, but when I was your age and in college, when stuff was bothering me, or I was down, it encouraged me not to give up. You're a young man now, and you have to start making your own decisions about what kind of relationship you're going to have with God," he said, putting his hand on my shoulder as we headed into the house.

I have to give my pops his props for helping me shake off the Rico Tate incident. Church ended up being pretty cool. Turns out it was youth day, and the choir was on point with their medley of Kirk Franklin songs. I was definitely feeling less disappointed with myself after that last tune that talked about believing in yourself and going for your dreams.

"And now I want to introduce our speaker for the day as we celebrate our young people," Pastor Simmons loudly announced. "Our guest is Mr. Charles Davis. He is the son of longtime members Mr. and Mrs. Charles Davis, Sr. He is a retired NFL player, from one of my favorite teams, the Washington Redskins!" Oohs and aahs rumbled throughout the congregation. "He's also the former owner of Flossin' Records and the soon-to-be owner of the Davis Rec Center." My eyes went wide and I perked up.

Chuck Davis was the man. He led the Redskins in passing and touchdowns during his entire career when he was a quarterback. He played for almost fifteen years. That's a serious career in football. Homie was up there with the likes of Brett Favre, Randall Cunningham, and the Redskins' great QB Doug Williams, who was the first African American to win a Super Bowl. Plus, Flossin' Records was one of the hottest record companies around when I was in junior high. I remember they had a lot of hot hip-hop artists out of the Virginia area.

"He's given his life back to God to serve the youth in our own church family and community, and he'll soon be opening the Charles Davis Recreation Center right here in DC," Pastor Simmons continued. "Please welcome Mr. Charles Davis." As he ended, the congregation applauded wildly.

Charles Davis, a well-dressed, clean-shaven brotha, sporting a nice piece of ice in his ear, standing an easy six-five, approached the lectern. His whole demeanor was laid-back, yet friendly, not what one would immediately suspect from such a big celebrity. Plus, he didn't seem like one of those *old* beat-down football guys. This guy was young and looked like he was up on some of that T.I. or T-Pain. Just knowing that he had been the owner of one of the hottest music labels in the country interested me. I wondered what his story really was.

"Today I want to speak to you about following your dreams!" He captured my attention right away with that line. "I want especially the younger people here to know that I had all the latest cars and bling bling, but nothing mattered more than my education! And I wouldn't have made it this far without prayer in my life. Now it's about giving back to you!"

People started clapping and saying "Amen," and I was actually diggin' what this guy was saying too, but I wanted to know more, and church definitely wasn't the place for questions. He really had a lot of positive things to say about staying focused in life, even when it feels like the odds are against you. When he finished talking, the whole congregation gave him a standing ovation. After church I was anxious to at least introduce myself to him.

"Excuse me, Mr. Davis?" I said, running up to him in the

parking lot. "I really liked what you were saying today. You look like you're still doing your thing," I complimented.

"First off, call me Chuck," he said, giving me a pound. "And I appreciate the good words. I guess you could say I *did* my thing. What I'm doing now with my foundation and my new work with the pastor is much more important than anything I've ever done before."

"What kind of advice can you give me if I'm interested in the entertainment business?" I asked.

"Wow, the business is definitely different than it was when I got in. You got the Internet, digital, just so many more components. It's no longer about just record sales. You really have to research and study the business and new trends. It's all about how you market what you're doing. Despite the fact that I was a sports celebrity, a lot of doors got slammed in my face before I had any level of success."

I heard my mom honking the horn. "Thanks a lot, Chuck!"

"You want to really thank me, come down and volunteer for me when I open my new rec center," he said, giving me another pound.

"No problem! I gotta get going, but I was wondering if I could talk to you more about the music business stuff too?" I was never one to be scared to go after what I wanted, and the one thing I did agree with my dad on is that a person has to seize an opportunity when it presents itself.

"We can definitely hook up. Here's my card. Give me a call!"

Chuck gave me his card, and I jetted. The whole ride home I started thinking about how I could really learn a lot from Chuck and get some tips on steppin' my game up to be a real future player in the entertainment business.

I glanced down at Chuck's card. It read: CHUCK DAVIS, CEO, THE POSITIVE DREAM FOUNDATION. That's whassup! I could be a CEO by the time I graduate next year. It's all about hookups!

Chilling out after Sunday dinner was family time in the Reynolds household, and I had been anxious ever since hearing Chuck Davis that afternoon to talk to my father about my future. My dad and I have a pretty good relationship for the most part. We even kick it like homies sometimes, watching sports, talking about world events. Sometimes we have really deep and thought-provoking conversations. The best part of our relationship is that we always keep it real with each other.

I waited until it was halftime. The Redskins were killing the Cowboys.

"Dad, did you know P. Diddy is worth fifty million dollars?" I said enthusiastically, like I was delivering late-breaking news on CNN or something.

"P. Diddy? Where did that come from? Anyway, that's ridiculous. But, hey, that's the day and age we're living in, I guess." He laughed, taking a glance down at the newspaper he had been reading on and off during the commercial breaks.

"I think he's a good role model."

"Blue, what are you getting at?" He eyed me suspiciously.

"My point is that he's no lawyer. He didn't even get a college degree!" I stated.

"Well, don't fool yourself. You're going to college! A little advice, son. How about you talk to me about people like Dick Parsons, the former CEO of AOL, or Ken Chenault, the head of American Express, and the biggest of them all, President Obama! Who, by the way, all attended law school! These are black men who understood education is the key to a lifetime of success. Not some hip-hop fantasy that gets you fast money. Those clowns waste thousands of dollars on diamonds for their ears and teeth! It's stupid, son. And what happens when you turn fifty? Do they have retirement plans for rappers, son?" he said.

"Dad, I'm not trying to be a rapper. I'm looking to discover talent and make hits. I want to start by giving club parties. I was inspired by that guy Chuck Davis in church today. So forget P. Diddy, even though he got his start giving parties too. Just look at Motown Records. You love that old stuff. Berry Gordy had a dream and discovered the Supremes and the Temptations," I stressed.

"And that was a long time ago, Blue. Times were different and a person could dream up something and just go do it. It was the era of dreamers. But nowadays dreaming is the quickest way to the unemployment line and no stock portfolio. Look, I can agree to you giving these parties on the weekends, maybe. I think it's a good idea for you to explore some entrepreneurial aspirations. But it better not interfere with your studies. Remember, high school is one thing, college is another. The real world is serious business, son.

"Getting a law or business degree makes you valuable in the economy today and in the future. Blue, with a law degree you can practice law, work on Wall Street, or work in politics, creating legislation and laws for clean air and energy. It's a solid foundation for a young man in today's competitive global workforce. You hear me? *Global*. Giving club parties doesn't open doors or your mind to the future," he said, turning the game back up as if there was nothing else to talk about. End of conversation.

My Sidekick vibrated. It was Whiteboy:

I'VE GOT A KID YOU MIGHT BE INTERESTED IN. IF YOU'RE DOWN WE GOTTA ROLL TO ANACOSTIA TOMORROW. HOLLA BACK!

I typed back:

FO SHO PLAYBOY! GOOD LOOKIN' OUT

Just the message I needed to get. Collin said timing is everything. He was right. There was no use trying to convince my pops of what my vision was for *my* future. I just had to do it. I had a hook now, and what my pops didn't understand was that the door and my mind had already been opened.

CHAPTER TEN

What becomes of a dream deferred?
It never makes it to the world to be seen or heard
—Talib Kweli, "Everything Man"

With my headphones resting on my ears, I sank deeper and deeper into the base line. Talib Kweli blasted knowledge into my eardrums. Eyes closed, head bobbing back and forth, I imagined standing onstage, rockin' out, in front of thousands of fans, black, white, Latino, Asian, one love, delivering a fresh freestyle over an illmatic beat. I am Nas, Talib, Pac, Snoop, Biggie, Jay, Kanye, *and* Weezy. I am the *next* one who will be crowned.

I was ready to spit fire. On the pad I scribbled down a few new lyrics:

"Martin had a dream, not deferred but heard he took his message to the masses they thought it was cool to shut him down but cain't no grave hold the soul of a street soldier down. So what

you gotta say, lost one? Betta watch what you say before you get shook, son. Before I load up this nine with knowledge and blow you away, son. God's my only judge. Man cain't hold no grave, no grudge. . . ."

I was just warming up, but suddenly I was interrupted by a hard tap on my shoulder. "Ain't this your stop, young?" I nodded my thanks to a laid-back West Indian dude wearing cornrows, gave him a pound, and exited the bus just as the doors were closing. I turned the volume back up on my iPod and made my way up the block, passing row house after row house, some neglected, others well maintained. Most of the people who own the houses around here have for years. People like my grandparents.

My grandmother, Corrine Lewis, who I call Sweets, is like a neighborhood icon. She's known for making pies and cakes. Sweets and my grandfather, who I call Pop Pop, have lived here over forty years. They used to own a bakery called Sweets Sweetbreads.

Back in the day this whole neighborhood was predominantly white, but in the 1950s it changed when all the black people moved here. Martin Luther King Jr. Avenue around that time, and for many years after that, was lined with businesses. Not so much of that now, but the annual MLK Day Parade is always poppin'. Walking through these streets is my daily routine.

Most people who live outside my hood think this is just

another ghetto community in America, plagued by excessive crime and drugs. But to me it's home. Everybody has a name, a face, and a mission, even the hustlas. Each brick tells a story.

"A-yo, Tre!" a voice buried in the middle of a group of guys hanging out on the corner shouted out. It was that white dude, the artist, Whiteboy. He was standing next to my homeboy Sauce. Some of the other neighborhood guys were hanging out too. Everyone was posted up on the corner chillin'. Whiteboy and I had planned to meet at my house, but here was just as cool. I was anxious to see what ideas he had about the CD cover for my demo.

Seeing what he did for Rook gave me the confidence that I needed to get serious about getting my music out there. I didn't have the cash to lock in studio time, but I was going to figure out a way. All I had was a few hundred dollars coming to me from doing that verse on Rook's CD. I figured hooking up with Whiteboy was at least a good start. Plus, he said he'd work with me on the price and bill me later. He works fast, too. I'd just hit him up yesterday. That's what I'm talkin' about. Why should I keep waiting to blow up?

As I approached the group, I noticed another dude standing next to Whiteboy. I had never seen him before. He was a clean-cut brotha who looked like he had stepped straight out of the suburbs. I gave a round of whassup pounds to everyone. All the guys from the neighborhood who hung out on the block were for the most part older than me. Some at least four or five years older. They're known as the block boys. Definition: cats who chill on the block. But the block boys are my peeps. They've been looking out for me most of my life. All I can say is, never judge a book by its cover.

A lot of these cats aren't thugs in the sense that they steal and kill. Some of them were once like me, students, hoping to one day make something of themselves. Unfortunately, they didn't have the right direction, and maybe went down the wrong path in life. All I know is the ones who do hustle are some of the smartest cats in math you'll ever meet. How else would they be able to flip drugs, make that cash, and triple their investments? That's street algebra and calculus. Word up! I often wonder why Wall Street and Congress didn't come down here seeking some advice or expertise before they gave that seven-hundred-billion-dollar bailout.

"Check this out, Young Tre," Sauce said, handing me a flyer. "I just started hosting a regular poetry and rap open mic at Busboys and Poets. I want you to stop through, anytime you want, and bless the audience," he said. Sauce was like a crazy blend of Asian and Jamaican, a former hard-head turned street preacher and poet. Getting the stamp of approval from him was like gospel around here.

"Good lookin' out, Sauce. Whassup, Whiteboy? Who's your man with you? I thought you were meeting me at the crib," I asked, checking out the corny, preppy-looking brotha with him.

"I saw my peoples Sauce and had to stop and holla at him. Anyway, this is my boy Blue Reynolds. He's about to be a major promoter in Silver Spring."

"Whassup, Tre," Blue coolly said, shaking my hand.

"You aren't from around here?" I asked, amused.

"Nah, Silver Spring." He smirked.

"You're a long way from home, B," I joked. "What you know about this, Prep School?" Laughter from the group erupted.

"Aw, don't trip. I'm up on Anacostia. My boy Whiteboy told me you were one of the dopest lyricists around." Blue was trying to impress me, but I wasn't mad. I was actually more flattered by the compliment.

"Yo, Tre, why don't you show Prep School how we get down around the way and lace the cipher real quick?" Sauce said, hyping me up. A cipher was when we all stood around in a circle and freestyled on the impromptu tip.

"Nah, man, sorry. I gotta holla at Whiteboy about some business, then head home and hit the books. You know my grandma be trippin' out!" I said, shaking my head.

"C'mon, Tre, just spit a little," Blue added.

On second thought, I couldn't disappoint the homies, right? A quick freestyle with the block boys, showing Prep School how we do it round the way, wouldn't hurt. Sauce started beat boxing, old-school style. Blue and Whiteboy were bobbing their heads.

"Yo, yo, yo, yo." I jumped, getting warmed up, and I was soon in the zone, spitting a quick verse:

"Anacostia is where I be from, where the heartless hustlas dwell. Most don't know, but most of these dudes is smart as hell. They just ain't lucky and end up in a jail cell. My streets sing the tears of Marvin. 'What's Going On' is what he once said. He preached a street soldier hymn of peace for these streets, but peace don't rest in these streets. And I know I'm a young hip-hop head, just tryin' to get ahead. That still don't mean I cain't ask why him and peace is dead?"

"Word that's whassup!" Sauce, Whiteboy, and Blue gave me pounds. The other guys joined in, some of the older ones even putting their hands on my shoulder, patting me on the back, tossing out various compliments like "That's dope, li'l homie." I was hood royalty. It feels good when the people got love for you. To my peeps around the way, I'm the li'l homie. I'm the hope that lives on their block.

They know I'm trying to do good in this life and make something of myself. Why the hell else would I wake up every morning at five a.m. to take the Green Line to Chinatown, then the Red Line to Dupont Circle, then hop off the Metro and onto the D2 bus. It takes almost two hours daily, to and from the Duke Ellington School of the Arts, but it's worth it.

"Thanks for the love. Peace out!" I said, giving a final round of good-byes to the corner crew. "So whassup, Whiteboy? You got my stuff!" I was eager to see the artwork he had been working on.

"Step over to the car. All the stuff is in the trunk," Whiteboy said, hitting a button to pop his trunk.

"Yo, just make sure you check out my open mic, li'l homie!" Sauce called out. I threw up the peace sign as we headed over to Whiteboy's car.

"Those are fresh!" I said, noticing his multicolored Nike high-tops.

"Just a li'l somethin' somethin'," Whiteboy said. "I always throw some work on my sneaks. Maybe one day I'll have my own line of sneakers or something."

"Hey, dream big, baby!" I said as we reached the car. He popped the trunk and pulled out some drawings that blew me away. My favorite was one that depicted me as an actual microphone. "This is it!"

"I'm glad you like it," Whiteboy said, giving me a pound.

"Yo, you got a lot of skills, Tre," Blue said. "Your flow is better than anybody out here signed or not signed, in my opinion. Maybe we could talk about doing some things together," he proposed.

"Like what? What's your story, B?" I said.

"Well, I'm launching a new entertainment brand," Blue said.

"Brand, huh? I like that," I replied.

"It's going to involve party promotions, but more as a way to showcase my artists, build a following, and expand to music on the Net, CDs—hey, maybe even merchandising or movies. The future is wide open!" Blue said.

"Word up? What other artists do you have?" I asked curiously.

"You'd be one of the first. The upside is that you'd set the standard."

"Hmm, maybe. But I'm really more focused on making my music and trying to get out a demo," I said.

"I feel you. Just know that when opportunity knocks, you gotta answer," Blue said. I'll give it to him, he was tight in his business approach. "So, what if I was able to hook you up on that demo action? That is, of course, if you're willing to sign with Blue Up."

"I'll think about it," I said, nodding. I was diggin' what Blue was talking about. I just wanted to make sure I didn't come off too anxious. Blue gave me a pound.

"I'd say this was a productive meeting. Think about Blue Up and think about these drawings, too. Don't sleep on my man here," Whiteboy said, rolling up the pictures and sliding them down into a cylinder. "You can hold on to these, Young Tre," he said, handing it to me.

"Cool! Look, I gotta bounce," I said. "But, Blue, I'll hit you back, or better yet, come check me out in Anacostia again. That is, if you can hang in the hood solo."

"Oh, I can hang!" Blue laughed.

"Cool!" I checked my watch. "Yo, I'm out!" I said, giving everyone a pound and turning to leave.

"Get back to me on that artwork," Whiteboy said.

"And get back at me, too," Blue said.

"I will, and, like I said, I'll seriously think about it!" I jetted.

When I reached my street, Maple View Place, I saw that the cops were a few houses away from mine, locking a brotha up.

Another one lost. Damn. It's crazy that you can see the Washington DC skyline from my block. It's actually kinda funny to me, since it mostly feels like we're the forgotten part of the city around here.

I can't help but be mad happy that the presidential election brought change. Maybe now people around here can get some love. But I ain't gonna get all political. I'm just letting it be known that no matter how much I blow up and how much paper I make, when I become the hottest rapper and producer, I'm never going to forget where I came from. I may even come back and build a performing arts school right here in Anacostia so kids don't have to take two trains and a bus to get to school every day. Word!

I unlocked the door, and Sweets yelled out to me from the kitchen, before I even got a chance to take my backpack off my shoulder. I placed it on the floor.

"Trevaughn, where have you been, chile? I was worried 'cause it was getting dark outside," she said, walking down the long hallway that led into the foyer.

"I'm sorry, Sweets. I was messing around with some of my friends up the block," I said, removing my jacket and hanging it in the coat closet.

"Oh, Corrine, he's damn near a man. These folks in this neighborhood look out for him," Pop Pop said, removing his eyeglasses. "Tre, you know she just likes to fuss."

"I heard that," Sweets said, turning back around before cracking a smile.

"By the way, Trevaughn, I have good news. I signed you up to be the new pianist for the young people's choir. We lost our pianist, but the choir director said you're more than welcome to play your guitar, too."

"That's great, Sweets, but I might be working on something really big, and I need to put all my time and energy into it," I said, glancing down at the flyer from Sauce.

"Son, what's so important?" Pop Pop interrupted.

"For one, I think I'm gonna do this open mic." Sweets hated when I talked about rapping or using my music to make hip-hop. "And for two, I might be recording a demo real soon."

"Trevaughn Antonio Martinez, I know you're not talking about that rappin' nonsense again. There is nothing more important than making music for the Lord," she said, putting her hands on her hips.

"Sweets, it's what I do!" I shouted out of frustration.

"Watch your tone, Tre," Pop Pop warned.

"Look, Trevaughn, you are a prolific musician on your way to a scholarship in music and academics—"

"I'm sorry, but, Sweets, hip-hop and creating music is my future," I said, cutting her off.

"I don't wanna hear another word," she said. I excused myself.

I sat down at my desk and pulled out the flyer Sauce gave me and pinned it to my bulletin board. I'm damn near a grown-ass man, and she'll see when I get me a record deal. I know one thing. If Blue Reynolds's word is on the up-and-up, I'm gonna get my chance to record my own songs. I don't care what Sweets or anybody else says. It's time for me to get my shine on.

I picked up my guitar and played a riff of guitar licks. I felt the tension release in my neck. I plucked another run of licks on some crazy Jimi Hendrix trip until my fingers felt like they were bleeding. I didn't even care if the music was too loud for Sweets and Pop Pop tonight.

CHAPTER ELEVEN

**I'm genuine with it
I ain't tryna put no pimpin' in it
—Chris Brown featuring Big Boi, "Hold Up"**

The day was starting off great. I got a text from Young Tre:

I'M DOWN WITH THAT DEMO

Yes! And I just got word back from Chuck Davis's secretary, confirming a meeting with him at the end of the week. My head was spinning, but in a good way. Everything was in motion. Now I had to step up to the plate for real. I followed up with Chuck, because to be honest, now that Young Tre was in, I didn't have a clue how I was going to make good on my promise. What did I know about producing someone's demo? There was no room for error.

In preparation for my meeting, I decided to take heed of Chuck's advice and get on top of that research he encouraged me to do. I didn't want to do my usual and cram. I wanted to take my time and really study the music business and the people who I most wanted to emulate. Chuck was a serious dude and, more important, a professional. I know Collin thinks I don't listen to him, but this time I was. I planned on being extra ready for my meeting.

I skipped lunch and went straight to the library to start researching everything possible about music moguls, past and present. Plus, I had a free period after that, so technically, I could get comfortable for at least two hours up in the spot! When I entered the school library, I suddenly felt like an alien in a foreign land. Let's just say that the last time I'd spent any real time here was freshman year. I know it sounds bad, but I've just had other interests besides the library. I sucked it up and got down to business.

After surfing the Net for about thirty minutes, going through magazine articles about some of the icons in the music industry, like Quincy Jones, Berry Gordy, and Clive Davis, my eyes felt like they were bleeding from reading so much material. I printed out one article in particular. It was about a man named Clarence Avant. They call him the godfather of black music.

He's in his seventies, but still a major player in the game, where he started out managing acts, owning record companies, discovering talent, the whole nine. He's known for his deal-making acumen. I envisioned being sort of like that dude. I also printed out some cool articles on Diddy, Jay-Z, and Jermaine Dupri. They seemed to be the youngest moguls making the business hot. I was set on the knowledge tip.

This library thing wasn't so bad. I decided to chill a little longer, and with the copies of those articles in tow, grabbed a stack of the latest hip-hop magazines—*Vibe*, *Giant*, *XXL*—and searched for a table. To my shock, Jade from the mall was in a corner, buried in a book.

"Errum," I said, clearing my throat. "Remember me? The rude guy at the mall? You're a hard woman to find."

"Yeah, okay, whatever, like you've really been looking for me." Our eyes met and there was an awkward silence. "So, um, what are you doing here?" she surprisingly replied, looking up at me.

"Studying," I said, clearing my throat.

"Humph. I've never seen you in these parts," she sarcastically replied. "Shouldn't you be at a party or something?"

I wanted to give her some smart-ass response, but she looked even more beautiful today. She had mad flavor on the style front, too, dressed in kneesocks, loafers, a miniskirt, and a pink and green argyle sweater. I was speechless.

"Hello?" she said, snapping her fingers like I was in some sort of trance. "You're actually blocking my light."

"Damn, do claws automatically come with that pretty face?" Touché! I had to come back hard. She rolled her eyes and started packing up her books in an attempt to leave. "Hold up. Can a brotha get a hello? I mean, you did come a little hard at me."

"Sorry. Hello," she said flatly.

"Maybe we should start over. It's Jade, right?" I said, extending my hand. "I'm Blue."

"Nice to meet you, I guess. I was merely giving you a dose of your own medicine," she said, shaking my hand with hesitation, but there was hope. I did get a smile out of her.

"Can I sit down over here?" I asked.

"Sure, I guess. It's a public place," she replied. I sat down in the seat across from her.

"I can't believe I've never met you. I mean, I know SSH has thousands of students, but I know practically every babe here."

"Babe? Are you serious? It's the twenty-first century. The women's suffrage movement is over. How about some respect!"

"Yo, can I ask you a question?" I asked. She cut her eye at me. "What's up with the tough-girl act?" I asked.

"No, let me ask you a question, Blue," she said, cutting me off. "Are you capable of not acting like a complete egomaniac and chauvinistic jerk?"

"I'm sorry," I said.

"Yeah, me too. Well, maybe this was a bad idea. The library is for studying, not talking! Maybe that's something that guys like you don't have to do. Or maybe you just come to school on the quest for new booty to get up in? I gotta go." She started packing up her books again.

"Wait, Jade. Look, I came at you completely wrong. I'm interested in getting to know you. Not only are you beautiful, but you're classy, smart, and despite how you just broke me down, you seem pretty nice." We both let out a laugh. "I'm really sorry for acting like an egomaniac and chauvinistic jerk. Isn't that what you called me?" We laughed again. "Can a brotha please get a do-over?"

"Yeah, sure, Blue," she said, shaking her head.

"Whew. Thank you. You *definitely* slammed a brotha. You know that, right?"

"Whatever."

"So, what are you studying?"

"I've got a biology exam in a few minutes. You don't look like the bookworm type, but I'm impressed. What are all those magazines and papers for? Or should I be scared to ask?"

"No, no. I'm doing some research on the music business. If you want something, you don't just have to go after it. You have to learn it and master it."

"That's cool."

"Yeah, like take Diddy for example. He went from interning at a record company to owning his own and producing records, as well as a multimillion-dollar clothing line, television shows, the whole nine!"

"You sound very passionate," she said, checking the time on her phone. "Hey, I've gotta go." Jade slid her tote bag over her shoulder and got up.

"I know I'm stepping way out there, but this is the second

time we've had to cut our time short. I don't want to miss another opportunity. Can I call you and take you out sometime?"

"Well, I'll give you my number," she said, scribbling it down on a piece of paper. "But I don't know about going out. I just got a job at Busboys and Poets after school during the week, and I really don't think I'll have time. Anyway, it was nice talking to you, Blue."

Jade smiled, and our eyes met. A brotha ain't trying to sound corny, but they sparkled. She had something special. They say when you know somebody's "the one," it's instant like that. I was determined to make her mine.

After school Collin and I headed over to Cutz and Tatz to hang out and talk about Blue Up. He was going to hear Young Tre for the first time and I was unveiling my plans to record a demo. Today would also be a bit entertaining, because Collin was going to take the plunge and get his first tattoo.

"Aiight. Until next time. Brilliant work as always!" Whiteboy's customer said as he walked out of the shop. His right pant leg was rolled up and he was limping slightly from the colorful, freshly etched collage of Chinese symbols Whiteboy had just etched into his leg. I could see the nervousness in Collin's face.

"Yo, you still wanna go through with it?" I said with a laugh.

"No, no, I'm ready to do it! No turning back!" Collin took a deep breath.

"Whassup! You holdin' up my schedule, playa! C'mon over

here and get in this chair. Man up!" Whiteboy teased.

"You know your pops is gonna kill you if he finds out," I said, taking a seat and picking up a magazine.

"Screw what he thinks. He doesn't even know I exist half the time," Collin said, unbuttoning his shirt and walking over to Whiteboy's chair.

"Those are strong words, homie," I said.

"Yeah, well, I'm just being real," Collin said.

"Then let's do this," Whiteboy said, wiping off a fresh needle.

"Just make sure that stuff is real sterile," Collin nervously stated. "And by the way, you got like some numbing stuff? I'm not real big on pain."

"C'mon, playa! What, you scared now?" I chuckled.

"Did you see that dude? He was in pain!" Collin's voice went up an octave when he pointed out the window at Whiteboy's customer, who was pulling off.

"Don't tell me you're punkin' out, young?" Dre, the shop owner, walked past, laughing and shaking his head.

"Hey, I ain't no punk. I'm just saying, I could get ink poisoning or something crazy," Collin said.

"Nah, Collin, I'm a professional," Whiteboy said, examining Collin's shoulder.

"Okay, now that we're done with the antics, let's get down to business. Collin, you know Whiteboy took me to see this kid named Young Tre, and he was incredible. I've got him and he wants to do a demo."

"A demo? Sounds cool, but how does that translate into you've got him?" Collin asked, squinting his eyes and turning away from Whiteboy's needle. "Ahhh!"

"Yo, I quit, Blue! I haven't even touched your boy with the needle," Whiteboy said, blowing out a puff of breath, holding up the tattoo needle in a surrender gesture.

"No, I'm gonna do it. I'll just close my eyes," Collin said, closing his eyes. Whiteboy shook his head.

"C, we're—Blue Up is—going to produce his demo. He'll be like our flagship artist," I said enthusiastically.

"Blue, I don't have a problem with you getting this kid. I defer to you on the creative picks. You have the eyes and ears, although I'd like to hear the kid. My concern is this demo part. When you say 'produce' that translates into Blue Up has to pay for something. All I see are the numbers," Collin said, motioning for Whiteboy to hold up.

"I hear you on that, but if we sign a kid like Young Tre to Blue Up, that would take our stock up. Remember when Diddy signed the Notorious B.I.G.?" I exclaimed. "We get a demo on him and we won't have to beg Rico for anything. He'll be begging us. Whiteboy, play Young Tre for Collin so he can feel what I'm talking about!"

Whiteboy placed his tattoo needle down and removed his rubber gloves. "You know I can't work under these conditions. Y'all are messin' up my flow. After this, no more interruptions!"

Whiteboy walked over to the stereo and slipped a CD in.

As soon as the track started pumping through the shop speakers, not just us but other patrons in the barbershop area started bobbing their heads. And then Young Tre kicked in with his verse:

"You still talkin' 'bout cars, clothes, and dough. I'm talkin' 'bout whatchu know. Knowledge is my dough. Spend that paper wisely, yo. Like Wayne say, blind eyes could look at me and still see the truth. Young Tre's the name, and I got nothin' left to say!"

"That's fi-yah!" Young Tre was taking me into the zone.

"Wow, he's definitely got something," Collin said, bobbing his head to the bounce of the bass.

"You like that? Hot, right?" Whiteboy smiled.

"Can you believe it? Fifteen years old, a kid from Anacostia, smart as hell, and we've got him! He's one of the dopest rappers I've heard since Tupac, kickin' knowledge with a crazy flow like André 3000 and Big Boi," I said.

"C, for real, when I met him in the studio the other night, I knew he had that *thing*. That's why I took Blue to meet him. He's young but vicious lyrically. I'm down for doin' the artwork for his demo."

"Rook ought to be nervous lettin' that kid rap on his CD," I said.

"Wack Rook!" Collin exclaimed.

"Okay, so let's say hypothetically you get this kid to sign to Blue Up, we do this demo, then what?" Collin said skeptically.

"We're giving him a shot. A shot to blow up. That's better than anything he has going on. We get Rico Tate to see how we're rollin'. He's blown away and gives us one of his spots to not only feature Young Tre, but put Blue Up in the club promotions game. We can even start looking for more artists.

"If Young Tre builds up enough buzz in our area and even in DC, we can get some major record execs to come in and see him, or shop him and get him a deal. They sign him and we secure a—cha-ching—distribution deal. We make the kid a star and we become stars!" I was envisioning it all.

"Slow your roll! All of those things are big ifs, and let's take one artist at a time," Collin said.

"Okay, you're the logistics guy. Work with me to make this happen," I challenged. "Look, can we do this demo or what?"

"How much is it going to take?" Collin shot the million-dollar question back at me.

"Based on what I researched, anywhere from fifteen hundred to two grand, but we'd need a producer, too. I've got about four hundred, maybe a little more, in my savings account," I said. "After the business cards, posters, and miscellaneous, we've got about two-fifty left from the money Whiteboy loaned us."

"I think I could come up with the rest. I should be able to get away with taking a grand out of the bank without my dad noticing. But I need a few days. His banker and I are cool," Collin replied.

"I can probably hook you guys up with some studio time,

and me and one of Rook's producers are tight. I'll tell him what y'all are workin' with, and he'll look out 'cause y'all are my peeps," Whiteboy added.

"Call the kid already! Let's put it in writing! And since we're on the subject of new talent, I went and checked out Mamie, also known as DJ Ill Mama," Collin said.

"And?" I asked.

"And she's pretty good," he replied.

"Pretty good or fi-yah good?" Whiteboy asked.

"That's what I'm sayin'. Does she have it like Young Tre?" I asked.

"I think so," Collin said.

"I don't know about coming out the box with a female deejay. We need a performer. But let's hear her demo."

"Well, she's working on a mix CD," Collin said.

"Hey, if she was serious, she'd have her music ready. In the meantime, we roll with Young Tre."

"Yo, if this meeting is adjourned, I got a tat to finish!" Whiteboy said, putting on a fresh pair of rubber gloves and picking up his needle to resume work on Collin's shoulder.

Twenty minutes later Whiteboy had created a work of art, as usual, on Collin's arm.

"Wow," he said, admiring Whiteboy's work in the mirror. The fancy script simply read FATHER. "It's kind of deep, don't you think?" We all agreed. I know the real deal. It's like Collin's been quietly wanting to rebel against his father for a long time. He had finally done something subtle, yet powerful.

"Oh, Blue, one more thing on Young Tre. I want to draft up an agreement. You just make sure he signs it. All we need is to pay for this kid's demo and he takes it to someone else," Collin noted, looking me in the eye. It's like the tat gave him a new confidence.

"That's whassup! I got a good feeling about this kid!" I gave Collin a pat on the shoulder.

"Ow!" Collin yelped.

"My bad, dude!" I said. Whiteboy started cracking up.

The three of us were still laughing and talking crap to each other and cracking jokes as we walked out of the shop. Whiteboy's back was to us as he locked the door and pulled down the security gate.

"I just want you clowns to know that I might be on lockdown soon," I bragged, typing into my Sidekick. I was sending a text to Jade:

I ENJOYED TALKIN 2 YOU 2DAY
HOPE WE CAN HANG SOON

"Remember babygirl from the mall, C? You know, the pretty girl in the audience at the homecoming dance, Whiteboy."

"You mean that stuck-up chick?" Whiteboy asked.

"Hold up. Mamie's girl, Jade? She hated you. You don't stand a chance with her," Collin said.

"No, we saw each other in the library, cleared the air, and I dig her. I think she's feelin' me."

"Oh, hells no, the library! That sounds like some straight sucka shit, young. I'm revoking your player's card immediately!" Whiteboy teased.

"Don't hate! Mamí gave me her number, and I'm not letting her slip away. Her girl's kinda fine too, C. You need to get up on that. She was all on you at the mall."

"Word? Babygirl is sweatin' you like last summer, C?" Whiteboy chuckled. "Sounds like you need to get up on that ass!"

"Mamie's cool. I think we could be great friends, but it's all business. Strictly *platonic*." Collin emphasized the platonic part.

"Then let me holla at her. I'll get up on that ass," Whiteboy said.

"Dude, she's not that type of girl! FYI, the caliber of girls you date might improve if you try to elevate yourself from that strip-club level of thinking." Collin had the serious verbal comeback. Laughter and high fives erupted.

"Oh, okay, you got jokes!"

Just then I was alerted to Jade's text reply. I read it aloud. "Yo, Jade writes, 'It was great talking to you, too. I hope to see you soon.' Oh, yeah! I gotta play this one right. She's gonna be a tough one to get, but I think I can do it. I dig her." I smiled.

"Sounds like Blue Reynolds is open," Whiteboy added.

"What! Fool, never that!" Whiteboy and Collin both shot me

one of those whatever-man looks. He was right. I was open.

We were almost to our cars when I noticed a tinted-out Ford Focus approaching. "Whiteboy, check that out!" I called out.

The car crept down the block and slowed to a stop in front of us. Whiteboy spotted the car and frowned. I'm not gonna lie. I know Collin and I stopped breathing. Whiteboy motioned for us to fall back.

"Just chill!" Whiteboy said, cautiously looking around.

"Nah, we got your back, man," I said nervously. The passenger window slowly came down and a clean-cut Puerto Rican dude wearing a Yankees baseball cap leaned out the window.

"Yo, who's Whiteboy?" he said.

"Who wants to know?" Whiteboy was cool with his response.

"Lopez!" he replied. "I heard Whiteboy's the best around town." Lopez pointed to the shop's sign.

"I don't know about the best, but I'm nice like that. Too bad the shop's closed," he said with a tense jaw. I played it cool, while Collin checked out Lopez's license plate.

"Too bad. Oh, snap. That's your Mustang, right?" he asked. Whiteboy nodded.

"I saw it at Rook's studio the other night, didn't I? You know I'm looking for him? He owes me something."

"Look, playa. I'm an artist. I don't roll like that. So, I got nothin' to do with Rook's business," Whiteboy said on the defense.

"I feel you. But you need to give Rook a message. Tell him it ain't over," Lopez threatened.

"Like he said, he don't roll like that." I was so heated that I couldn't sit back and keep my mouth shut any longer.

"Your boy got a big mouth." Lopez shot a threatening look at me.

"He ain't got nothin' to do with nothin'! Look, I heard you, amigo. I don't think I'll be seeing Rook anytime soon. We good?" Whiteboy was letting Lopez know he needed to move on.

"Yeah, we good, amigo!" Lopez said before motioning for his homeboy driving to pull off.

As soon as the car was out of sight, Whiteboy lit into me. "Don't ever open your mouth like that again, B! This shit ain't no joke. These fools out here are killers," he shouted.

"Well, if we say we got each other's backs, then that's what I was supposed to do!" I said with intensity.

"But you and Collin ain't from the streets. There's a code out here," he said.

"Let's just get outta here. Are you okay?" Collin asked.

"Yeah, I'm straight," Whiteboy said, opening his trunk, tossing his backpack in, and slamming it shut. "I just get heated that as much as I try to get away from that life, it's bullshit like this that keeps you on edge," he said.

"Can't we call the police or something?" Collin asked. We gave him a look. My boy was showing his whiteness. He was definitely not up on the "code of the streets." Even I knew that.

"The police don't care about cats like that rolling up on us," I said.

"I ain't no snitch! I just gotta keep my distance." Whiteboy gave us a round of pounds.

"Aiight. I'll holla," I said, hopping into the driver's seat of my car. Collin jumped in on the passenger side. I slid Young Tre's CD in. I pulled out my wallet and showed Collin Chuck Davis's card.

"See this, C?" I said, holding up the card. "I know sometimes it doesn't seem like I listen to you, but I do. You always help me see things more clearly, and I realize going after an artist for Blue Up isn't going to be easy. Knowledge is power, and this is exactly the knowledge I'm going to tap into so that we can do this thing right.

"I've got a meeting with him to get some guidance on this music business thing, especially since we're going to have our first artist in the studio soon. This guy's a former NFL player and was the owner of Flossin' Records. He's a serious baller. Hey, I'm all about resources," I said. We gave a fist pound on that.

"Just remember to get that contract signed once I type it up for you," Collin reminded me. "Oh, and wish me luck," he added as I started the car.

"For what?" I asked.

"It's my dad's birthday and his secretary scheduled a late dinner for us at the Four Seasons in Georgetown."

"Damn, playboy, is that how the rich folks do it?" I joked.

"Yeah, whatever. Let's trade places."

"Anytime, C!" I put the car in drive, turned up the volume on Tre's song, and pulled off.

I was already over that crazy encounter, thinking about my next mission: getting the money together to put Young Tre with the golden flow in the studio.

CHAPTER TWELVE

COLLIN

I refuse to be a bum
Especially coming where I'm from
—N.E.R.D., "Provider"

I printed out a short form agreement that made Young Tre exclusive to Blue Up for ninety days. Since we weren't offering him any money or a concrete record deal, I figured that was fair. Worst-case scenario, we invest in his demo, get nothing for him, and stomach a loss of at most a couple grand. It was fair business and more of a win for Young Tre, but business is a gamble, right?

Before jumping in the shower, I got an urgent message from Mamie:

I GOT THAT HEAT FOR U. DEMOS READY.
MEET ME @ THE SPOT LATER

This was great news. Even though Blue's focus was on Young Tre, I still believed Mamie could be an asset to Blue Up. Getting her message was also motivation for my dinner with my dad. I really wanted it to go well. It was his birthday, and we'd finally get a chance to just relax and maybe talk for once. I may even tell him about Blue Up.

Usually he's working in his study, or I'm leaving as he's coming in. We barely communicate, but I knew once he saw all I was doing, he'd be proud. I stood in front of the bathroom mirror and admired my tattoo. FATHER. I smiled at my reflection.

Yeah, I just needed some time. I could make my own moves as a lawyer, and who knows. Blue Up could become a major entertainment company one day. I smiled again.

My hands were sweaty and clammy as I nervously tried to decide whether or not to go with the red tie or the blue one. Screw it! I went with the blue striped one. My dad would think the blue was much more professional and more fitting for the atmosphere at the Four Seasons in Georgetown.

I got dressed and did a final check in the mirror. Then it was time. I was sweating bullets. I was about to *finally* open the envelope with my SAT score in it. I purposely didn't even go online to look it up. I knew I couldn't open it without some help. I raced to my herbal stash. A blunt would really take the edge off. I opened the small wooden box I kept in the back of my closet. Damn! I was all out of weed. Note to self: *Alert Whiteboy it's time to call his connect for a refill!*

I grabbed the envelope and my car keys off the dresser, slipped my Sidekick into my suit jacket pocket, and jetted downstairs. I had an hour before dinner, and a little liquid courage would do the trick. I unlatched the door to my dad's glass liquor cabinet and pulled out the bottle of Grey Goose vodka, grabbed a glass off the rack, and poured myself a generous shot. On second thought, I made it a double. I dropped two ice cubes in the glass, took a long swallow of vodka, and slowly opened the envelope.

Sweeter than *sweet*! I practically leaped off of that stool. I'd scored a 2300. A perfect score was 2400. Not bad, Collin Andrews. *I'll drink to that!* I said to myself, taking a sip. I glanced down at the score again. Kick ass! Nothing was stopping me now. I checked my watch. I had to bolt or I'd be late. I didn't even have a chance to call my mom. Wait until my boys get the news. They're gonna flip! I downed the rest of my drink, placed the bottle neatly back in its place, and was out, feelin' pumped and buzzed!

I'd been sitting across the table from my father for fifteen minutes, but barely ten words had passed between us. I felt a lump in my throat and beads of sweat forming across my forehead. My hands were clammy again. I needed another shot of vodka and *two* blunts to get through the rest of the evening, for sure. My father was busy checking his BlackBerry messages. I looked over the menu at least twice more before breaking the silence to make my announcement.

"Dad, I have great news. I got a 2300 on the SAT. Pretty good, right?" I stated proudly. My father just looked at me, silent. The only noise from our table was the sound of him closing his menu. "I, um," I stumbled, clearing my throat. "What do you think?"

"Well, at least you have plenty of time to take it again," he said, cutting me off. I was stunned. "I gotta tell you, a 2300 is far from a perfect score. You obviously didn't work hard enough," he said, taking a sip from his glass of Jack on the rocks. I felt the expression on my face hardening.

"The better news is that I made a few calls, and this came to my office yesterday," he said, handing me an opened letter.

I read the first words on the page: "Congratulations, Mr. Collin Andrews." Georgetown had selected me and nineteen other students from around the country for a special summer program for high school juniors. I would be one of only two students from the DC metro area. I'd spend four weeks in the dorms at Georgetown taking pre-law prep classes, listening to guest legal professionals, and meeting some of the students.

"I just hope that when you go up there to Georgetown, you take the time seriously. This is going to be great on your high school résumé. Now, I know the head of the law school, and I don't want to be embarrassed."

"Dad, the Georgetown program sounds great, but didn't you hear *me*? I just gave you great news. Can you at least act like you're a little proud?" I was starting to shake with anger. "I may as well have gotten a 100 on the exam. You would've reacted the same way!" My voice was starting to get louder.

"You watch your mouth, Collin. What about your gratitude for what I did for you? And by the way, you'd be smart to learn how to take criticism. It's going to be there at every corner of your career."

"Dad, I don't have a career yet. Maybe for once I just want to have a decent conversation with my father. Sometimes I wish we had what Blue and his dad have."

"With all due respect, how Dave handles his son is none of my business, but if you ask me, he's the reason that kid's all over the place. I'm not gonna give you an inch. You hold a kid's hand too much, they'll never be able to stand on their own and fight the corporate beasts out here. You want warm and fuzzy, get it from your mother," he said, angrily removing his glasses and taking another sip from his glass.

"We're not the same, me and you. You may be embarrassed by my test score, but I'm ashamed of *you*! Thanks for dinner, and happy birthday, but I lost my appetite," I said, staring him dead in the eye, tossing my napkin on the table.

"Collin, I'm warning you," he threatened with a tight jaw. "Don't you dare get up from this table and embarrass me."

"I've already done that, *Father*," I said, standing up and walking away without looking back.

* * *

My text from Mamie read:

WHERE U @

Half a bottle of Grey Goose later, I stumbled slightly into the Spot. Mamie was hanging out there listening to music. The room was spinning. I leaned against the bar and felt a light tap on my shoulder.

"You made it. Late as hell, but thanks for at least coming." Mamie smiled. She looked hot in a white tank, tight jeans, and red stilettos.

"Damn, you look good." My words were a little slurred, but I was still in control.

"Um, okay, whassup with the freshness. Anyway, like I said in my text, my demo's ready. Plus, I talked the owner into letting me do a little set so you could check me out live and in living color. I gotta see when they're gonna let me go up," she said, turning around and ordering a bottle of water. I kept my eyes on her backside. And then it was too much to resist. I grabbed her ass and pulled her close. "What the fuck, Collin!" she said, jerking away.

"Yo, I'm just buggin' out. My bad!" I said, grabbing her bottle of water and taking a gulp.

"Collin, I don't know what's going on with you, but it ain't cool."

"Hold up. First of all, you sweat me to come down here, and

now you wanna act like this. Fuckin' bitches kill me!" I said, throwing my hands up in the air.

"Look, you're drunk, and lucky for you I'm gonna let that foul shit slide!" Mamie angrily grabbed me by the arm and dragged me outside.

"What the fuck are you doing," I said, stumbling backward.

"Collin, I'm going to drive your sorry ass home. I'll just get my purse and my CDs and I'll be right back. I can do a set another time. Don't move!" She ran back in the club.

Nervous energy was all over me. I felt the sky caving in. I was sweating and clammy. All of a sudden, everything I had eaten in a week was on the sidewalk. The thought of my behavior disgusted me and was sobering. I guess I passed out after that.

"Here, drink this," Mamie said, shoving a piping hot cup of coffee in my hands. Somehow we'd made it to her house and were sitting on her bed. "Thank God my aunt worked an all-nighter at the hospital or you would've been up shit's creek, sleeping on the concrete."

"How did we get here?" I asked, rubbing my pounding head.

"Fool, you passed out, and I had to get Big Mike, the bouncer at the club, to help load your ass in the car. My car's in the shop, so having yours there was the only positive aspect of the night. You showed your ass. You know that, right? I couldn't believe how you were talkin' like some fake-ass busta."

"Mamie, I wasn't myself. I'm going through some tough

things right now. I guess I thought Grey Goose had the answers to my problems."

"To be honest, I *was* surprised," she said softening a bit. "It seemed like your boy Blue would've been the one acting more like an oversexed, sloppy-drunk fool." We both found the humor in that.

"Oh, yeah, you tried to grab my butt and everything. Not cool. Not cool at all."

"My bad. I'm really sorry again. I would never do anything like that."

"Oh, I ain't hot enough for you now?"

"Don't get me wrong. You have very nice *ass*-sets, but stealing a feel isn't my thing," I said. We shared a laugh. I suddenly felt nauseous again.

"Oh, God, here!" Mamie held a small garbage can up to my face. I dry heaved. "Humph. I guess it's all over the sidewalk in front of the Spot. Lie down. You can get yourself together and I'll get you out by seven, before my aunt gets home. You're in no condition to go anyplace. But you do owe me, big-time."

"Anything," I said, lying back on her bed. The room began to spin. I put my hands over my face.

"Here," she said, placing her demo CD on my chest.

"You gotta listen, and I'm telling you now, it's dope. Put me down with Blue Up. I need a break, a *real* break," she said, taking a deep breath. "Look, Collin, I don't know what it is about you, but it seems like you have good intentions. Not too many people have ever looked out for me, especially family. My own father didn't have my back. I need this opportunity."

"I know what you mean about family," I said, holding the CD in the air.

"Your parents together?"

"Divorced. My mother lives in the Hamptons."

"Oh, shit. Y'all rollin' like that? Damn, must be nice. You got brothers and sisters?" Her question was painfully sobering. I was at a loss and didn't know how to answer her.

"Let's just say money doesn't fix everything. My father's what you might call an asshole. Look, I don't like talking about my family."

"Hey," she said, patting me on the hand. "Join the club. You should get some rest."

"Mamie, thank you."

"That's what friends are for. We are friends, right?"

"Absolutely!" I made myself comfortable and closed my eyes. The room was still spinning. Mamie rubbed my head, but it was in an innocent way. For the first time in a long time, I felt like someone really cared.

CHAPTER THIRTEEN

**World famous, we ain't nameless
—Mos Def, "Freestyle"**

"I guess you underestimated me, Tre. You didn't think I'd come to Anacostia alone, huh?" I said as Tre and I drove down Martin Luther King Jr. Avenue, headed to Tre's house. I turned onto his street, parked in front of his house, and got out.

"Nah, man. I thought you was one of them regular corny suburbia cats. I'll give it to you, it takes heart to come to the hood, not once, but twice!" Tre said as we walked up the steps to his porch. "Check that out over there." He pointed toward the DC skyline.

"You can see the Capitol building from here," I said in shock.

"Yeah, but with all those brains, Congress, lawyers, judges, they can't fix the lives of people right in their own backyard."

I really was diggin' Tre's logic. He was two years younger than me, but this young brotha was intelligent and focused. It was like he was wise beyond his years.

We entered the house, and the smell of apple pie baking made my mouth water.

"Trevaughn, is that you?" Tre's grandmother called out.

"Yes, ma'am. I've got someone I want you all to meet in the living room," he yelled back. "Man, living with your grandparents is crazy. I love them, but old people have funny ways. I can't play my music too loud or video games on the TV in the living room. And my grandmother has this thing about Vicks VapoRub."

"Word?"

"Yo, if you have a sore throat, she'll put some Vicks on your throat. If your foot aches, she'll put some Vicks on it. If you have a headache—"

"Don't tell me she'll put Vicks on it!" I said.

As our laughter died down, his grandparents joined us in the living room. It was showtime, and I was eager to get to business, and so was Tre. I didn't pick up Tre from the Duke Ellington School of the Arts in Georgetown and drive him home all the way to Anacostia for the view. No, I did it to get him to sign a contract with Blue Up.

"Sweets and Pop Pop, this is Blue Reynolds, the guy I was telling you about, and, Blue, these are my grandparents, Mr.

and Mrs. Lewis." The three of them sat on the couch, and I sat in a chair across from them. The moment was somewhat intimidating.

"Mr. and Mrs. Lewis, I think your grandson is a tremendous talent," I said, taking a deep breath.

"Son, I know that. Most importantly, the Lord knows it." Mrs. Lewis frowned.

"Sweets, give the young man a chance to explain himself," Mr. Lewis said, patting her on the arm.

"Thank you, sir, errum," I said, clearing my throat. "I'm here because, as I told Tre, I'm building a music and entertainment empire, and I want him down as the first artist at the future home of Blue Up Productions. I'd like to get your permission to sign up Tre," I said, pulling out the contract Collin drafted. He was so smooth he had even created Blue Up Productions letterhead.

"Listen, son, Trevaughn is a minor, and although I don't like the idea of none of this nonsense, he speaks highly of you. But that don't mean two beans to me. Trevaughn has obligations at church, and he's a straight-A student. And furthermore, you don't look a day older than him. I wanna know how some high school student has money to have his own *empire*. Humph! We old, but we ain't stupid. I got dinner cookin'," Mrs. Lewis said, storming off to the kitchen.

"Sweets!" Tre called out. "Pop Pop, do something. I want this!" Tre pleaded.

"Young man, a lot of people see a talented person like Tre and want to take advantage of him, and our priority is making sure Trevaughn is protected."

"Sir, I know I'm young, but so was Berry Gordy when he created Motown. I'm not here to sell you all a pipe dream. I know you were once young and may remember having an idea, and all you needed was that push. Well, I'm that push."

"This boy's got a chance to go all the way, and school is the priority. We want him to be a doctor one day," Mr. Lewis stressed.

"Sir, just know that all I'm asking for is ninety days. Ninety days, and if I don't make something happen, then Tre's free to go," I said, handing him the contract.

"Let me work on his grandmother and we'll get back to you. I like your determination, young man," he said, shaking my hand and then exiting the room.

"Blue, come look at something," Tre said, leading the way to the front door. I was down. As we walked up his street, I could see the clear difference between his house and some of the others.

"Some of the people around here have owned these houses for years, and they take pride in them. People like my grand-parents. They look to me to make something of my life and get out of here one day. But then you got some people around here who've gotten swallowed up by poverty. They get on that crack and get smoked out, and some are just triflin'," he said.

As we walked I got an even better idea of what kind of person Tre was. He had his mind right and a plan for himself too.

"I guess you're showing all this to let me know that you gotta be true to your roots and what you represent?"

"I'm showing you this so you know I ain't in this for show. I'm fifteen and I've seen more shit around here than cats twice my age. I gotta make it out. I promised my grandparents and my parents," he said, pointing toward the heavens. "But I'm never gonna sell out! Feel me?"

"Yeah, I think I do." I nodded.

We headed back to the house and decided to finish talking on the front porch.

"Look, Tre, I've got the money, and come tomorrow I'll have the studio and a producer in place to record your demo so we can get this thing poppin'. I trust your word, but my partner needs me to get something in writing since we're putting our time and finances on the line. I hope you can convince your grandparents."

"You just keep that studio time. My word is my bond. Somebody from around the way tried to come at me before. They wanted me to sign my life over. Sweets gets real nervous about contracts. I'm in, but you gotta take my word this time. I'll sign the paper when things calm down."

"It's business, but I'll trust you on this one," I said, giving him a pound and turning to leave.

"I wanna know why you chasin' a cat like me down so hard."

"I knew you were a star. That's from my heart for real," I said.

"Then I'll keep it real with you. Losing my parents when I was just a kid made me stronger, if that makes any sense."

"Perfect sense," I said. "Let me help you show the world who Young Tre is. We could be huge."

"Trevaughn, time to eat dinner!" his grandmother said, peeking out the front door.

"I gotta go!"

"Thas whassup! Hey, don't forget that contract. I'm counting on you!"

The entire drive home my mind was racing almost as fast as the traffic around me. It was all really happening. Blue Up was going into the studio to make its first demo. My Sidekick buzzed. It was Collin. I was dreading his call, because I knew exactly what he wanted, but I didn't *exactly* have it.

DID YOU GET IT SIGNED

I hesitated, then typed back:

IT'S ALL GOOD

CHAPTER FOURTEEN

WHITEBOY

**Never mind what haters say
Ignore 'em 'til they fade away
—T.I., "Live Your Life"**

"Mr. Tommy James?"

I was mad nervous, and the lanky, nerdy dude sporting long stringy hair had to call my name twice to get my attention. I quickly put away my sketch pad, where I was putting the final touches on my idea for the Blue Up logo. I got up and followed him into a well-lit art classroom. Not too many people call me by my government name. Ms. H is really about it.

"I'm Peter Mason, the associate professor of art here at the Art Institute of Washington. We really liked the material you submitted with your application. That's why we wanted you to come in for a one-on-one interview," he said, shaking my hand, before proceeding to give me a whole speech on the school. I

had read about it in the newspaper and then went online to find out more.

I didn't know much about going to school period, but I did bust my ass to get my GED. I guess listening to Blue and Collin talking all the time about college and stuff got me hyped. Now, with Blue and Collin working on Blue Up Productions, I wanted to have my game together too. On the real, when you got peeps around you who are positive, it makes you wanna do positive things.

Unfortunately, I had straight zoned out. My nerves were rocked just sitting here in the classroom. The more this dude talked, the more nervous I got.

"Can I see your portfolio, Mr. James?"

"Excuse me?" My heart was pounding.

"Your work, your drawings, please," he said, reaching for the portfolio I had placed on the table when we walked in. I decided not to tell my boys and to keep all this to myself for now. I just didn't want to jinx things. I mean, I've had so many disappointments in my life that I just don't get all pumped up about shit that could fall through. I swear if I'd had a fat blunt, I'd have blazed up right now. I must've been crazy driving all the way over here to embarrass myself.

"Mr. James, may I ask what inspired this piece?" he said, holding up a copy of the picture Juice painted on my car. I smiled.

"That's dedicated to my grandma."

"You must be very fond of her. The angel wings are so detailed. Wonderful!" His compliments had me feeling like I'd come here for the right reasons. "What about this one?" he said, holding another picture up.

"It's a charcoal sketch I call *Lost Ones*. Actually, it's like a self-portrait," I said, lowering my head. I remember drawing that picture when I was in a real dark place. Things were so bad I wanted to straight commit suicide. I wasn't gonna be no punk about it either. I was gonna take a nine and go straight for the dome. *Blaw!* A bullet through the brain. I just didn't want to think anymore.

When I look at all my drawings, I think about how far I've come. I made it through some bad shit, growing up with a mother who was drunk, out of her mind most of the time. I was just a kid, watching her crawl out of her own vomit and piss. I never knew my father. I went from foster home to foster home. It was like trouble followed me. I did it all—fighting, stealing, selling drugs, carjacking. I ain't never killed nobody, though.

"I just didn't have anything to live for when I did that," I said, looking at the picture one last time. "I guess actually drawing it out kept me from doing something crazy," I said somberly. "I was blessed to have my grandmother, even though she died before she got to see me change."

"Well, thank you very much."

"That's it? You don't need me to like audition or anything?" I asked.

"No, Mr. James. We'll be in touch."

I felt like I had wasted my time. I had to get up outta this spot before I straight punched the dude.

I needed to blow off some steam, so I stopped by the pool hall to play a few games. I just wanted to forget about art school. It was a dumb idea. I got ready to rack up the balls, and who rolled up on me but Lopez. This day sucked!

"Whassup, playboy?" he asked.

"Yo, I told you I can't help you out with Rook. I ain't seen him," I said, lining up my shot.

"Somehow the cops been sniffin' around where I live, asking about a robbery that supposedly I was involved in."

"Playa, you're tellin' on yourself. I don't know nothin'," I said, standing up straight. I hadn't been pushed in a long time, but I could hold my own. "I ain't no snitch!"

Lopez backed up and made sure to flash me his gun before leaving. I suddenly wasn't in the mood for pool anymore. Today hadn't turned out how I planned at all. I can't catch a break. The only thing I wanna do is live my life right! I slammed the cue stick down on the table and jetted.

CHAPTER FIFTEEN

**All you see is videos and shows
But there's more to my life . . .
—Usher, "Follow Me"**

The week had flown by and today was my meeting with Chuck Davis, but before heading to his house, I made a pit stop at Collin's to pick up the money for Young Tre's studio session.

"Wow, I can't believe we're really doing this!" Collin excitedly pulled out a stack of hundreds and counted it out. "Five, six, seven, eight, nine hundred, a thousand!"

"Good news," I said, reaching into my pocket. "I had more than I thought in my savings account. I was able to get five hundred, and with Whiteboy's money that makes seven-fifty!"

"Sweet!" Collin excitedly replied as I combined all the money and counted it out. For several minutes we stared at the money that was spread out on his huge granite kitchen countertop. I took a deep breath while the whole scenario sank in.

"This feels so major right now. What if Young Tre's music really blows up?"

"Then we're outta here, dude! Oh, by the way, here's Mamie's mix CD. I think it's great!" he said, reaching in his backpack, which was hanging on the back of a nearby chair. "You won't be disappointed."

"Time to make some hits, baby," I said, holding up the CD. "It's all about Young Tre. I'll listen to your girl when I can! We're set for tomorrow at Right Trak Studios in Takoma. Whiteboy's got it all arranged and will be there with the producer cat." I gathered the cash and stuffed it in my wallet and gave Collin a fist pound before exiting. It was on!

When I rolled up to Chuck's estate in Chevy Chase, Maryland, I was blown away. I thought Collin's house was the bomb, but it didn't compare to this one. My house in Silver Spring is only about three miles away from the town of Chevy Chase, but damn, what a difference a little more zeros in the bank ledger make. This is exactly what I'm talking about, working hard to play hard.

I know I'd only met the dude once, but just after hearing him speak briefly, it seemed like he's living the life I definitely want. More important, he seems supersmart. Chuck has made some great business moves. I did my homework and Googled him already. Flossin' Records had all the hot artists back in the day. He didn't do so bad getting a couple Bowl rings with the Redskins either. Maybe he even had to go against his parents to prove himself.

I sat patiently in what I've heard the ballers on MTV's *Cribs* refer to as the "grand room." This cat had real class. I probably could learn a lot from him.

"Hey, Blue! I'm sorry I kept you waiting. Let's talk down in the chill room. My wife likes to keep things too neat in here," he said. We shared a laugh.

"Thank you so much for meeting with me," I said as he led me through the foyer and down a long hallway. We finally ended up in a room off the kitchen. I could understand why they called it 'the chill room.' It was the ultimate spot to chill out.

A large leather sectional that could probably seat ten easily dominated the room and gave prime viewing to the flat screen television. That joint had to be at least seventy inches. Bang & Olufsen stereo system, full wet bar, and the massive amount of sports memorabilia in a glass-enclosed case. The view was a pool and basketball court. Crazy!

We parked ourselves on the couch, and I could barely contain my questions. "Chuck, this is exactly how I want to live. I feel like I'm in an episode of *Cribs*! Did you get all this from owning Flossin' Records or from playing in the league?"

"Look, Blue, I like your energy and flavor. So I'll make a deal with you. I'll tell you my secrets to success if you promise to really listen," he said in a serious tone, leaning into me.

"Word is bond!" This was going to be great. "Chuck, I'm all ears.

"But first, I want to know what's your story? What are your plans after high school?"

"Well, I have one more year to really solidify my plans. I figured I'd get more serious senior year. In the meantime, I'm building a company I just started, Blue Up Productions. I want it to incorporate promoting club parties and events, but also developing artists, managing them, making music for the Internet—hey, maybe even Internet content. It's all wide open. I'm just hoping to get some tips from you! The downside is that my dad, who's a pretty successful lawyer, is on me hard about following in his and my grandfather's footsteps. He even wants me to go to the same college," I said.

"And what do you want?"

"Basically, I just want to be able to do what you did so that I can have all the cars, rock the jewels, and a home like this. You know, blow up like you."

"Sounds like you got it all together."

"I also have an artist already. His name is Young Tre. He's like Tupac meets Outkast. I've got his music. Do you mind listening to it and telling me what you think?"

"I'm honored that you value my opinion. But before I listen to it, I want to explain some things. First of all, don't be fooled by this material stuff. I may have gotten by MBA from Columbia, but I got my real degree from the school of hard knocks. Flossin'

Records was the worst business decision I ever made. Sure, we had some hit records, but because I didn't know how to manage a business and didn't have the education or skills to do so, I practically went bankrupt," he said. I was shocked.

"I didn't see all of that on Google!"

"Maybe you didn't dig enough, or that's proof you can't believe everything in the media. I had a great PR team, constantly cleaning up my mess."

"But you're not broke now. I don't get it," I questioned.

"Young brotha, you gotta pay attention." He laughed. "When I was drafted into the NFL, I didn't listen to my parents and I went on a spending spree. I ended up in so much debt my dad had to sell his business to bail me out. Then when my career was on the rise, I started makin' paper again and decided I was going to be in the music business.

"So I went into further debt to invest in a bunch of so-called artists who spent more time partying, drinking, and smoking weed than making a profit in record sales. The moral of the story is that I took the long, stupid, and expensive way to getting to where I am. When I met my wife, she helped me get on track to go back to school and get my degree, and now I have the knowledge to make the right decisions. I had to rebuild my life. I don't want you to make that mistake. Having said that, let me check out this talent you've got." Chuck placed Tre's CD in the stereo and pressed play. All I had was the song he had recorded with Rook, but I burned a copy with Tre's verse.

When the track came on, I could tell Chuck was lukewarm, but once Tre's vocals kicked in, he closed his eyes and started bobbing his head and tapping his foot to the beat.

"Wow, he's the real deal."

"I'm putting him in the studio to do a demo, and then I want to put it in the hands of this guy Rico Tate. I'm hoping that will get me access to his venues so I can throw parties that feature talent like Young Tre."

"Rico's a pretty important cat. You certainly shoot for the top, don't you?"

"I'm young and new and probably inexperienced, but I got drive and ideas that I think would benefit a guy like Rico Tate," I said confidently.

"Listen, I know Rico very well, but you've got to come correct. You could get him interested with what you just played me, but it's nice to know you're thinking ahead and are going to get the kid a real demo."

"Yeah, I learned that about him the hard way. I never got an actual meeting, but I did approach him and kind of blew it. Actually, I embarrassed myself. I tried to go up to him in public and it was a disaster."

"Just remember, most of us so-called ballers blew something when we were starting out."

"Do you think you could hook me up with Rico Tate?"

"We happen to be good friends. Let me see what I can do, but my name and reputation would be on the line to a certain extent. I'd advise you to get the hottest track you can find for this kid to rap on. I can tell you Rico's all about what makes people dance in the club. Also, know what you're looking for from a deal standpoint. Be short and to the point with him. All that matters is how much money he can make."

"I won't let you down!" I said, giving him a pound.

Just then Chuck's BlackBerry alerted him. "Hey, Blue, I've got to end our meeting. It's my architect. I need to go check on the site for my new community rec center. Keep in touch, and you owe me some volunteer time with the kids once I get it up and running," he said.

"No problem. I appreciate the conversation," I said.

"I also want you to really think through things before you put your education to the side. The only way I see you truly having success is that you *learn* your way."

"Huh?" I said.

"You've heard of *earning* your way. Well, my philosophy is that you use education to help you build your empire. Just know life isn't about glitz. It's about the grit you put into it. That's when you see the real results. Think about it, and consider me a resource, a mentor even," he said, giving me a pound. Then we hopped into our respective cars. His was surprisingly a low-key Ford Explorer. I was expecting a Bentley or a tricked-out Range Rover.

Later that night, lying in my bed, I started recapping my conversation with Chuck. The pressure was on and I was feeling somewhat nervous. Sure, he was willing to possibly call in a favor to his buddy Rico Tate, but the key word is "possibly." The ball was rolling now, and if I didn't hit a home run with Tre's music, I'd be over before I started. I shook it off and picked up my Sidekick and typed a quick note to Jade:

JUST THINKING ABOUT U

Seconds later she hit me back. Her message read:

**EXHAUSTED FROM TONS OF HOMEWORK
BUT HAPPY TO HEAR FROM U.
START WORK 2MORROW. GOODNITE.**

I had the biggest cornball grin on my face, but it was all good. Jade's reply made me forget about being nervous, and was the perfect ending to a dope-ass day.

CHAPTER SIXTEEN

So many days I've thought of you
It's about time you knew the truth
—Amerie, "Why Don't We Fall in Love"

Busboys and Poets was an eclectic café in midtown DC. It's located in an area that used to be mainly black, but with all the gentrification, the neighborhood is multiethnic, urban cool. It's the kind of place where you'd find a mixture of artsy and scholarly types. People came for the food but mostly for the chai teas, conversation, and to chill with the cool kids.

The restaurant features everything from weekly poetry open mics to book signings, live music, and even political roundtables. I never thought I could actually have fun on a job, but it certainly seems like there's never a dull moment around here. My girl Mamie had pulled it off again and gotten me a part-time waitressing job during her shift. Mamie was a straight hustla,

just like she had hustled and maneuvered a slot to spin classic funk and soul music for an hour during her shift.

"Girl, quick heads-up, sometimes the night-shift manager, Miss Shante, wears eye makeup and lipstick. So, don't find yourself staring," she said, making one final warning before putting on her apron and being swept up in the café's buzz. I couldn't understand why she was passing that little tidbit of info on, but whatever.

"Okay, cool," I replied.

"Good luck, and make some money!" She smiled. We high-fived and she was off to take orders. Meanwhile, I stood awkwardly waiting for our boss to show up.

"You must be Jade!" I heard the piercing crack of a semi-deep voice, and spun around. My immediate supervisor, Sean, towered over me. "Everybody calls me Shante, dollbaby!" Sean—excuse me, Shante, as *he* prefers—blew me a series of air kisses, then slapped an apron into my hands. He was not only wearing full makeup, but a hot pink turtleneck and black leggings. I ain't mad. Sean—I mean *Shante*—had the legs of life! Thank God Mamie had already warned me. Working here was definitely going to be wild, but I will say that Miss Shante was totally cool, but a totally insane bug-out!

Every table in the place was filled, and apparently the dinner rush hadn't even hit. "Whew! Here's your pad, and pencil," he said, handing me the items one by one. "Today's special is lentil soup and grilled salmon. You've got section three. Never try to work another person's section, no answering cell calls while waiting on a customer, feel free to grab a bite on your break, but don't break longer than fifteen minutes, the evening crowd kills us, and no frolicking with coworkers during business hours. Got it?"

"Right, sure, I think," I answered with a confused look. I suddenly felt completely overwhelmed after that crash course in waitress dos and don'ts.

"Well, chop, chop, precious. We've got hungry customers!" Shante said before sashaying away.

"Girl, get the lead out of that booty. You've got two tables waiting to give orders," Mamie whispered frantically before whisking a veggie burger away to an eager table.

"Pick it up, Miss Jade!" Shante barked as she led a large group to my section. I felt a meltdown coming on.

Thirty minutes later I was finding a groove. The short rush had cooled off, but I had another three and a half hours to go. Shante was setting up the stage in the front of the restaurant.

"Hey, chica, are you surviving?" Mamie gave me a pep hug.

"Barely," I replied, scooping my hair up into a ponytail.

"You might want to fluff that hair and put a little shine on those lips. Look, three o'clock, ma! It's Collin and Blue."

"What are you talking about? Oh, my God! How do I look?" I said in a panicked tone.

"You're fine. Damn, he is really diggin' you to show up at your job and thangs."

"Yeah, I guess. I kinda like him, too."

"Good, 'cause I need you to whisper sweet nothings in his ear about my music. He's bullshittin'. Collin is on it. He just gave my mix CD to Blue, but Blue's busta ass hasn't listened to it yet. They supposedly have to focus on doing some demo for this rapper kid. It would be nice to work on that."

"No problem. I'll ask him about it and push him," I assured her. Mamie gave me air smooches before rushing off to pick up an order.

I fluffed my ponytail and did a quick application of lip gloss before making my way over to their table.

"What a surprise," I said, holding my pen and pad.

"I was thinkin' about you. You remember Collin, right?" Blue said.

"Hey, Jade, good to see you," Collin said.

"You too. By the way, my girl is going to kill me if I don't find out right now when you guys are going to listen to her mix CD."

"Soon, I promise. I've just gotta clear my plate. We're taking our first artist in the studio—tonight, actually. I'm gonna hit her up soon," Blue said.

I noticed Miss Shante cutting her eye at me. "Uh-oh. I'd better take your order before I get fired."

"A chai tea latte," Collin replied.

"Make it two, and I'd love to give you a ride home. By the way, a couple of menus would be nice." Blue smiled.

"Oh, my God. I forgot! My bad. Coming right up, gentlemen, and nice the way you slid that whole ride-home thing in." I smirked.

"Miss, I need to place my order," an impatient male patron called out.

"Miss, we've been waiting a long time too," another disgruntled voice called out. Right now would be a good time for that *ding* from the Southwest Airlines commercial to sound off, alerting me that I was free to run up outta this joint. I rolled my eyes and quickly rounded up the other orders.

Within minutes I had returned with the lattes.

"Two chai tea lattes," I said, placing them on Blue and Collin's table. "What do you want to eat?"

"Looking at you is enough." Blue had a way with words, and as corny as his line was, I started to blush. "So, when you get off would you like to go by the studio with me? Blue Up's first artist will be there recording his demo."

"I don't think so. Mamie's car is in the shop and I'm riding the Metro with her."

"Why doesn't she come with us too!" Collin said.

I think Mamie was more excited than I was when I told her we'd be going by the studio. Something felt slightly groupie-ish about the whole adventure, but, hey, you only live once!

Two hours later our shift was over and Mamie and I were surprised to find Collin and Blue parked outside of the café asleep in Blue's car. I banged on Blue's window, startling them. We had a good laugh before jumping in and speeding off to the studio in Takoma Park. When we arrived, I was shocked. All there seemed to be were old abandoned warehouse-looking buildings. Blue pointed out the address of where we were going.

"Right Trak is back here. Follow me," he said, grabbing my hand and leading us down a short alleyway. I was skeptical. I always thought the music business was more glamorous.

Inside, there wasn't much either, but the room that housed the actual studio was kind of cool. There were computer screens set up and a large mixing board with all kinds of sliding buttons and speakers everywhere. In front of it was a big glass window, and on the other side a microphone was set up.

The session was already in progress.

"Yo, Whiteboy!" Blue motioned for a heavily tattooed guy to come over. He didn't look much older than us, but he certainly didn't look like your everyday high school student. He had a hard-core bad-boy edge to him. "This is Jade and Mamie," Blue said. "Ladies, this is me and Collin's homeboy, Whiteboy."

"So you're the one who's got my boy open," Whiteboy said, and chuckled. "It's nice to meet you, ma."

"Damn, he put you on blast, Blue," Mamie teased.

"And you must be the deejay. I heard your skills were nice," he said, licking Mamie with his eyeballs.

"Whiteboy, huh?" she said, giving him a playful look.

"Yeah, yeah, he's the type of guy your mother told you to stay away from," Collin said, stepping between Mamie and

Whiteboy and showing us over to a nearby couch.

"Whatever, hater," Whiteboy said, tossing Collin a friendly middle finger.

"Damn, Whiteboy's kinda hot," Mamie whispered in my ear.

"Girl, please, you always go for the bad boys." We both giggled.

As I watched Blue move throughout the small studio, I found myself captivated watching him. He and Collin huddled with Whiteboy and the producer—they called him Loc—who had just arrived. Loc sported long dreads and had dark shades on. Mamie swore he was high. Then a guy who was about five-eight, somewhat lanky, but muscular, entered. His close-cut curly hair and big smile gave him a boyish look.

"Tre! Whassup! You've gotta meet my partner, Collin!" Blue shouted. The guys gave each other a series of pounds before Blue introduced Tre to me and Mamie. "Jade and Mamie, meet Tre, aka Young Tre!" It was all love, and then the action started.

Tre was reserved and low-key. Not to sound stereotypical, but I guess I was expecting him to be the wild rapper type. Blue had hyped us up about Young Tre's skills, so both Mamie and I were anxious to hear him get on the mic, Mamie especially.

Loc hit a series of buttons on the massive sound board, and the bass from the track pounded through the large speakers surrounding the room. My whole body vibrated.

"Personally, I think it's kinda wack," Mamie whispered, twisting her mouth. I wasn't crazy about the track either, but what did I know. The song had that Southern feel, like the old songs rappers like Master P made.

"I'm not really feelin' it either," I said.

"I know my music is ten times better. Blue needs to put me down, girl."

When Young Tre stepped into the booth and started spittin' his rhyme, it was like the whole room came to a standstill.

"*Check one, check two, yo, yo, yo. Martin had a dream, not deferred but heard. He took his message to the masses. They thought it was cool to shut him down, but cain't no grave hold the soul of a street soldier down. So what you gotta say, lost one? Betta watch what you say before you get shook, son. Before I load up this nine with knowledge and blow you away, son. God's my only judge. Man cain't hold no grave, no grudge. . . .*"

It didn't matter that the track was weak. He was the bomb. Mamie was buggin' out, inconspicuously pinching me.

"Ow!" I yelped.

"Girl, I could lace Young Tre with one of my tracks!" she said, rolling her eyes.

I wanted to stay longer, but I still had homework to do. I motioned for Blue to take me home.

"I'm sorry, but it's getting late. I have to get home," I said when he leaned into me.

"No, it's cool. Collin's gonna drop Mamie, and I can take you now," he said, helping me up. I was impressed by Blue's attentiveness.

Outside, I gave my girl good-bye hugs, but not before she made sure to give Blue some words. "You need to quit playin' games. My music is dope, Blue. I could hook your artist up," she said, throwing her arms in the air in a what's-up-with-that gesture.

"I got you. As soon as I get things rollin', I'm gonna get at you for sure," Blue called out. She waved him off as she and Collin drove away.

"Blue, she's really good."

"I'm sorry, but she's unproven, and right now I've got to break an artist. I've got some major players lined up and waiting. I'm not trying to play your girl, but that guy Loc has worked with everybody from Yung Joc to Bow Wow." I know he was sort of blowing her off, but I was dog-tired, and all I wanted to do was get home. On the real, I'd had my fill of Mamie and Young Tre.

I must've passed out, asleep, right after I gave Blue my address. The next thing I knew I was parked in front of my apartment building being awakened by Blue.

"Wake up, Jade," he said softly. "You want me to walk you up?"

"No, no," I said, collecting my purse. "I'm fine," I said, whipping out my keys.

"My moms would kill me. Every gentleman walks a young lady to her door," he said.

"It's cool. Just wait for me to go in before you pull off. Well, bye." I gave an awkward wave, slamming the passenger door shut.

I was halfway up the stairs when Blue shouted out, "Hey, do you think I could take you out on a *date* date?"

"Sure!" I yelled back without even turning around. What he couldn't see was the size of the smile covering my face. When I got inside my apartment, I exhaled. I giggled to myself, intrigued by the thought of our *date* date.

CHAPTER SEVENTEEN

It's gravy baby, I got it all smothered
—G-Dep, "Special Delivery"

I stopped by Right Trak Studios and met up with Loc and White-boy before my date with Jade. Loc played all three of the songs he and Tre had been working on, and I wasn't feeling any of them. After a full weekend in the studio, we were squeezing the last bit of juice out of our seventeen-fifty.

"Loc, I just need you to put more heat on these tracks, you know. Give me that Kanye club feel!"

"That ain't my style, young. I'm more that Southern screwed sound. That's what's hot. Plus, you ain't payin' me Kanye dollars, fool." Loc was getting upset.

"Yo, Loc, chill. My boy's just tryin' to get that club hyped banger. Give me a minute," Whiteboy said, eyeing me. "Blue, let me holla at you," he said, pulling me over to a nearby corner.

"Whiteboy, your man isn't giving me what I paid for," I said with frustration.

"B, you paid him less than his normal two grand, and he's doubling as a producer and engineer. Trust me, you're getting what you paid for. Now, I agree the songs aren't much better than the track Tre did with Rook, but this is what we got to work with."

"Maybe, maybe not," I said, with a glint in my eye. "Can you play something for me, Loc?" I asked, racing over to my backpack and pulling out Mamie's mix CD. He slid it in the CD player, and when the beat dropped, the combination of Go Go percussions, heavy bass, and energetic tempo was a sound so fresh I was blown away.

"Whiteboy, all the elements are there, and it's good, but it needs some work," I said, taking off my jacket and sitting in a chair next to Loc behind the mixing board.

"Work that shit out. I gotta bounce. I'm doin' a tat for my boy who works for Santana Moss of the Redskins. I've been tryin' to get at Santana to hook him up. This might be my in. I'm out!" We gave each other fist pounds, and I got to work.

Although I had never produced a song in my life, my natural instincts took over. I had Loc sliding dials on the board and punching in keys to program the drumbeats. You would have thought I was the second coming of Jermaine Dupri, or Timbaland, rolled into one. Loc laid Young Tre's vocals in, and I had my hit. Mamie had created something special, but by the time I finished rearranging the track, it was perfect. It's like taking a skeleton and putting meat on the bones. Actually, I was the meat, so I probably didn't even have to worry about giving her credit. Besides, she was a no-name, some obscure little deejay. It was all good!

I pulled up in front of the public library just as Jade was walking out. It was her day off, but she had a major paper due. I actually had to write a paper for history, so our date would be short. The most important thing was seeing her, and that was going to be worth staying up all night to finish my own home-work. I was leaning up against the car when she approached.

"Don't think I'm gonna make it a regular habit of going out on heavy homework nights, Blue. How am I going to get into medical school that way?" she said, giving me a friendly hug. "So, where are we going?"

"Does it matter?"

"It might," she replied coyly.

"Trust me." I guided her over to the passenger side.

"No, really, where are you taking me?" she probed. I winked and closed the door.

I don't think I knew myself where I was taking her. I just wanted to be with her. We ended up in Georgetown.

"Oh, my God, I love it here," she said.

"Yeah, it's cool over here," I said as we strolled down the main road lined with all the trendy shops—Urban Outfitters,

H&M, American Apparel, which was my favorite spot to get fresh sneakers.

"I dream about one day being able to shop at all these stores. When I'm rich enough to buy one of these houses, that is," she said, looking around. Georgetown was upscale and definitely the place to be seen and spend cash.

"Maybe one day I'll take you shopping, Jade," I said, putting my arm around her.

"Blue, I don't need you to buy me anything," she snapped.

"Okay, first off, we're gonna have to work on that tone." We both laughed. "Second off, me wanting to take you shopping is because I want to lace you up, do things for you."

"Is that how it always is with girls you date? You 'lace them up' to perhaps impress them enough to make them give you the ass?" Jade smarted.

"I don't date a bunch of girls, contrary to what you think. I like you, and I want to get to know you better. I told you that. I'll go as slow as you want, but damn, babygirl, if I wanna buy you something, it's not because I want some ass or anything else from you. I can get sex if that's all I want," I said, looking into her eyes.

"What do you dream about, Blue Reynolds?" she asked.

"C'mon. I'll show you," I said, grabbing her hand.

As we sat on the waterfront of the Potomac River, we could see the Washington Harbor, the famous Kennedy Center, the Washington Monument, and clear over to Virginia.

"You still haven't told me," she said.

"Told you what?" I said, cutting my eye at her.

"Stop playin', Blue! What do you dream about?"

"Okay, okay. Well, I've read about all those dudes like Jay-Z and Diddy and Russell Simmons, and even back to people like Berry Gordy, the man who created Motown Records. It's like their hustle was insane. Each of those guys had a dream to make incredible music, and they made their fortunes that way.

"I'm not a musician, and outside of Jay-Z being a rapper, neither were any of them. It's about your vision and having that business mind to know that you can find talent. Just like the show *American Idol*. Simon's no musician, but his instincts tell him when someone's a hit. I got instincts, strong ones, and even my pops has always told me that I've got a natural knack for deal-making.

"You could have all the talent in the world, but who's got the vision to take you to that next level? I could come up with more innovative ways to stream an artist's music on the Internet, make even more successful clothing lines, produce movies. I could make global superstars and parlay this whole party-promoting gig into an empire.

"Damn, I probably just bored you to death," I said, feeling insecure for the first time. Jade really had me open. I told this girl who I haven't even known very long the things I hold closest to my heart.

"I wasn't bored. I was really taken by what you said. I just hope you can help Mamie. Did you listen to her music yet?"

I suddenly felt a sharp tug in my gut. Maybe I should tell her that I listened to it already, but then she'd probably get so excited, she'd call her girl right now. I couldn't deal with Mamie's questions about the CD. I had Young Tre's future in my hands. I didn't have time to explain the whole scenario of using her track, fixing it, etc. Sometimes things in the music game have to go down like this. It's not personal. "Yeah, I promise to look out for your girl at some point," I said, clearing my throat. "Um, I may even listen to her CD tonight."

"Thank you so much, Blue," she sweetly replied. Damn, I really hated lying to her, but business was business.

"But let's get back to us. I really value your opinion. You sure I'm not making a fool of myself talking about all my dreams and stuff?"

"No, I feel like you're being real with me."

"So what do you dream about, Jade?" I asked.

"To blow up, like all of us want to. I want to be a doctor, be successful so that I can, for a change, take care of my mom. I'm all she has. Wow, I needed this conversation more than you could ever know, Blue."

"What's wrong with her?" I asked, putting my arm around Jade.

"It's nothing. She's just got surmounting medical bills, no insurance, blah, blah, blah. Don't get me started. I'll sound like a broken record."

"That's what I'm here for. For you to vent," I said.

"Not much else to say. I've just always dreamed of being a doctor, and she's my main motivation. I never knew my father. He's black. That's about all the info I have. One day I'm going to find him, though. I promised myself. My mother doesn't want me to, but it's something I need to do," she said, wiping her eyes.

"You think you could be down with somebody having your back for a change?" I said.

"I think I would like that very much," she said, and smiled.

I knew Jade was different from the moment I saw her. First off, she didn't take any crap from me. It was like she was her own woman, confident and beautiful. She wasn't like the other girls at school. They were all about getting with a guy who could give them a high-end lifestyle, and they were gossipy. She's not even on Facebook? Damn, I think I found a keeper.

I couldn't help myself. I put my arms around her and pulled her close, kissing her deeply. Damn, she could become addictive if I wasn't careful. Then I just held her close and we watched the boats go by. Just like Bonnie and Clyde, Jay-Z had his Beyoncé, and now I had my Jade. That's whassup!

CHAPTER EIGHTEEN

MAMIE

**When I grow up, I wanna be famous
I wanna be a star, I wanna be in movies
—Pussycat Dolls, "When I Grow Up"**

"I sure hope your man hurries up and listens to my CD, 'cause I'm ready to make some real money. All this work is for the birds!" I told Jade, ringing up a to-go order.

"He promised to listen. You just have to be patient. He gave me his word he was going to get at you. It could happen really soon."

"Okay, okay, him having it is at least better than nothing. Being in that studio the other night was the best. It gave me confirmation that all my dreams aren't in vain. I know my tracks are better than that guy Loc's. It may take me a little longer, but I'm going to keep chipping away. And don't worry. I'm not going to stress you out over Blue. I know you'll look out for me. It's all good, and I'm so positive about all this that I think I'll go get some inspiration at the Spot tonight. Wanna go?"

"C'mon, girl. I don't know why you keep asking me. I don't club. I study and work," she said, giving me a playful shove.

"Well, you might want to change your mind one of these days. The owner just sent me a text, and their regular deejay's out sick. So guess who's filling in for her first full set?"

"Oh, my God! Oh, my God! I'm so there. I've got tons of homework, but who cares!"

"Girly girl, get ready to be blown away by yours truly. Holla!" She high-fived me.

Since the café was slow tonight, our boss let us off early, and Jade and I made it to the Spot with plenty of time for me to get ready for my big set.

"Girl, I'm so nervous," I said, setting up my records for tonight. My heart was racing. I looked out over the dance floor. The Spot was a quaint laid-back lounge, but tonight it was packed.

"Stop it, Mae. You're going to be awesome."

"I don't know. I'm used to getting up here for five, ten minutes max, but an hour nonstop, I just don't know. What if I'm not that good, or just not as good as I think I am?" I said, wringing my hands. "I'm gonna tell the owner I can't do this."

"Mae, listen to me," Jade said, grabbing me by the shoulders. "Girl, you've come too far and been through too much crap to quit."

"I know. I guess it's just, you talk something up so much, and when it finally happens, it's like, 'Damn, this is for real.'"

"Tonight is just a start. Once the word gets out, you're gonna blow up, girl. Now, if I didn't believe in you, my ass would not be here, 'cause you know how I am about my studying. So, what's up? You gonna punk out?" Jade said, challenging me.

"Hell, no, I ain't gonna punk out! Get outta my way. I'm ready for my close-up!" I threw my arms around her. "Thank you, Jade, for giving me a pep talk and having my back."

When I dropped the needle on the record, I transformed into Ill Mama.

"Whassup, people. I go by the name of Ill Mama," I announced, fading in the beat of a neo-soul track. "Tonight I'm gonna keep it smooth and not only give you what you want, but what your soul needs. Shout out to my girl, Jade!" She knew I had to put her on blast. Jade definitely held me down tonight. "This one's for you, *mamacita*! And to all the other fly sistas out there workin' hard to come up out here, this one's for you!" I brought the music back up and turned the Spot out.

That hour zoomed by, and my set was so tight that the owner told me I was officially the backup deejay from here on out. Yes! I guess the struggle was finally paying off, sort of. At least I thought everything was all good. I should've known there would be some crap from my aunt Deb when I got home.

✳ ✳ ✳

"Do you even know what time it is? On a school night, no less," she said, standing in the hallway.

"I'm sorry," I said, noticing that the clock on the television screen that was still flickering with some late late-night program read one thirty a.m.

"'Sorry' just isn't cutting it anymore, Mamie. I can't deal with my job all day and then have to come home and worry about you all night. I didn't know if something had happened to you in the club you hang out in or what. What do you have to say?"

"I don't really. I was checking out some music at a club and I got a chance to spin for an hour."

"Did you forget that you are a high school student? Hell, I don't even know if you're that anymore. You could've dropped out since our last conversation about this, for all I know."

"I haven't dropped out."

"This is your final warning. We have got to come to a meeting of the minds and respect this house or I'm going to wash my hands. You'd better get on top of going to school and doing the work ASAP."

I stood expressionless for a few moments, then trekked off to my room. I was trying not to hear all this in the middle of the night.

CHAPTER NINETEEN

BLUE

I don't plan on goin' broke, put that on my Maybach
—Rick Ross, "Maybach Music 2"

I had no idea what to expect when Chuck sent me a text:

PLS BE AT THE REC CENTER SITE @ 6
FOR A MEETING WITH RT AND
BRING YOUR GAME FACE

It was like I'd been waiting my whole life for this moment. I shot a text to Collin and hopped in my mom's car and jetted off to Chuck's office. I was going to meet Rico Tate, and Chuck had set it all up.

"So, Blue, I kept my word. I told you I'd set you up with Rico, but I hope you thought about all the things I said when we

were at my house." Chuck and I were sitting in his unfinished office at the rec center, waiting for Collin and Rico to arrive.

"Most definitely. After talking to you, I understand now more than ever that this is not a game. You gotta be smart and strategic. I think you helped me see the light," I said.

"Now, that's what's really up!" Me and Chuck gave each other a hearty fist pound. "But I'm not letting you off the hook. I'm going to be staying on you about the importance of that college degree. Just know all the parties and the material things will all be waiting for you when you put in the work!"

Collin knocked on the open door.

"C'mon in. You must be Collin," Chuck said, reaching his hand out.

"Yes. Mr. Davis, it's great meeting you. I'm Collin Andrews, Blue's partner!" Collin was shaking Chuck's hand so hard I thought it was going to break off.

"Collin, no worries. You don't have to be so formal. I'm on your team." Chuck laughed, offering Collin a seat next to mine. We gave each other a pound. "I've got to take care of some important calls, but Rico will be here shortly. We have a meeting to go over final construction. Let me know what happens. Chuck left me and Collin sitting like two balls of nerves. We looked at each other with fear, not sure what was going to come through that door next.

Moments later Chuck walked Rico into the room. He and Chuck greeted each other like old buddies.

"Rico, this is the young man I was telling you about, Blue

Reynolds, and this is his partner, Collin," Chuck said as Rico sized up both of us.

"Yeah, I remember this one well. He almost got my driver, Snake, upset. That could be bad for a person's health," Rico sneered. "Listen, like I told Chuck, I'm a busy man. I only have a few minutes. I want to be clear. I'm taking this meeting only because he and I go back and I trust him. I hear you want to roll in my league, Blue."

"Yes, sir." My heart dropped to my stomach, but I had to keep my cool. This moment was too big to blow again.

"What makes you think you're up to the task?" Rico wasted no time focusing in on me. Collin sat in silent support.

"Well, sir, um, success is all about opportunities. Opportunities are granted by people who somebody else gave an opportunity. I'm looking for you to give me mine." I swallowed hard and cleared my throat.

"And?" Rico replied.

"And I'm a proven tastemaker with today's generation," I said confidently.

"Nothing you're saying means anything. How do I make money?" Rico's swagger was bordering rude, and I was ready to say forget all this. I didn't need to jump through hoops for anybody. Plus, I felt like I had been set up to fail in this meeting. Chuck was sitting back watching me fumble.

"Look, Mr. Tate, Blue's creative instincts are fresh and innovative," Collin said, jumping in to do the recover move. He nudged me hard. I took a deep breath and decided to give it my best.

"My instincts are what led me to launch what I call a new brand in entertainment. It's about knowing what's hot before it even hits, tapping into the trends and creating a go-to destination for teens. Teens who, by the way, spend not only their parents' dollars, but their own. Blue Up is the future."

"Is that it?" He folded his arms across his chest.

"Okay, the reason why Blue Up will be a successful venture with you is because I will personally treat everyone who walks in the door of a Blue Reynolds affair like they're VIP. My partner, Collin, is my eyes and ears throughout the club.

"The philosophy at Blue Up is all about making our guests feel like they're experiencing something for the first time, every time." I was ready to go toe-to-toe with Rico. "Our parties will cater to the under twenty-one, but these are the next generation of movers and shakers. That upscale, young, flashy, and classy crowd!"

"So, what attractions do you have?"

"Huh?" I said with a confused look.

"Who's your star power if I give you one of my venues?"

"That's a great question. His name is Young Tre," I said, reaching into my backpack and pulling out Young Tre's unfinished demo. I handed it to Collin.

"I've heard him, Rico. The kid is real nice." Chuck was finally coming to bat for me. Rico nodded.

"We've got this incredible kid who's gonna be the next Kanye, but better. He brings the neo-soul meets old-school hip-hop vibe.

I'm looking to launch him at our first exclusive event. He's going to be huge!" I was on a roll.

"And what else?" Rico questioned.

"Well, sir, we're lining up more talent," I said.

"May I?" Collin asked.

"Go for it!" Chuck replied. Collin pressed play on the stereo, and I crossed my fingers.

"Put on the fourth track. It's not mastered, but you'll get a strong feel for it," I said, giving Collin the go-ahead.

When the drums, bass, and horn samples kicked in, I thought Rico Tate was going to jump up and start dancing.

"That's enough," Rico said, regaining his cool and standing up. Collin and I were dumbfounded. We thought he was diggin' Young Tre, but he told us to turn it off. He reached over and gave Chuck a pound and proceeded to exit. Before opening the door, he turned back around.

"Mr. Tate, what did you think?" I asked.

"Kid's good, real hot. I wanna see the kid live."

"There's a regular open mic at Busboys and Poets. I could put him up there for you to check out."

"Here's my card. Let my secretary know what time and when. Let's see how that goes first, and if he's as good as that CD, you've got Club Toast next week. Seventy-thirty is the best split you'll get from me, and I'm the best. Oh, and I might need a copy of that track! Who produced it?"

"Um, I did," I boasted. Collin shot me a look. "But, um, see, it's not quite ready yet," I nervously replied. "You know, sample issues."

"Make sure you let me know when it is. It might be worthy of some club play," Rico said.

And just like that the meeting was over. I guess the expressions of shock on me and Collin's faces were priceless, because Chuck got one helluva laugh. Chuck told us to let ourselves out since he had to run to another meeting.

"How great did that go?" I said, reaching out to give Collin a pound as we walked out of the rec center. He halfheartedly reciprocated the gesture. "What's up with you?"

"Blue, the meeting was great until you played Young Tre's demo. First off, I didn't know it was done. Secondly, that was Mamie's track. Which is great, but we didn't get her permission, and you *didn't* produce it!"

"Collin, you were studying and we were in trouble with Loc. He just wasn't giving me what we needed. So I pulled out Mamie's CD, and it was hot. I didn't have time to run it past you or her," I said defensively. "Look, I had the vision. I made the track better. Don't sweat it. I told him he couldn't have a copy. Hey, all I did was what Diddy would do!"

"That's bullshit, Blue! You aren't Diddy!" Collin said, raising his voice.

"Instead of arguing with me, you need to be trying to get Tre's songs online so we can generate even more hype."

"I'm not comfortable with this legally or personally."

"C, you aren't a lawyer, and neither am I. We're hustlin' right now. Everyone will get theirs in due time. This is about Blue Up blowing up. Okay, I'll compromise. For now, we'll put some of his other stuff online that Loc did to get a buzz going. Then once we wow Rico at open mic, we'll hit the Net with the track I just played him. That'll give me time to figure out what to do about Mamie."

"What if Mamie hears it?"

"Damn, C! Can't we just focus on gettin' that bread? We'll cross that bridge when we get to it," I replied. "Plus, you're all worried. Who knows, after all my work, she might not be able to tell it's her track."

"She's my friend, Blue. All you had to do was call her."

"Call her and then what? I wasn't trying to consult with her. Yo, this is business! Friend or no friend, just forget about the no-name female deejay for right now. Look, I'll hit you later!" I was out. It didn't matter we were this close to Blue Up becoming legit. Young Tre would be the deciding factor. I had to tell him to alert his boy Sauce that he was going to do open mic.

CHAPTER TWENTY

All I need is one mic . . .
—Nas, "One Mic"

I felt my cell buzzing. It was a text from Blue:

OPEN MIC @ BB'S AND POETS TOMORROW.
I GOT A MAJOR PLAYER COMIN
2 CHECK U . . . RICO TATE

Word! This must be that snowball effect people always talk about.

"Tre, you okay, son? I'm just saying good night." Pop Pop knocked lightly on my bedroom door.

"I'm great! Blue delivered. I'm supposed to perform at this place in midtown tomorrow. The only problem is that's choir rehearsal."

"You really want to do this, don't you, Trevaughn?" he asked, sitting down next to me.

"I want this, Pop Pop, and it means a lot that you always step up for me. I guess I wish Sweets was more supportive. As long as I'm doin' my music and I can feel it in here," I said, pointing to my heart, "it's for God, and it doesn't matter if I perform it in church, or in this café, or in the club. I love performing *my* music, and I've got a chance to do that tomorrow. I need this shot, Pop Pop."

"You gotta do what God gave you the gift to do, son. I guess you'll be needing a ride, huh?"

"You have got to be the flyest grandfather in the world," I said, giving him a pound and then a hug.

There wasn't an open seat in the joint. I'd never heard of Busboys and Poets until Sauce gave me that flyer. The room was overflowing with love and artistry. Seeing just how serious other cats were about their craft, and on the flip side, how receptive the audience was, opened my eyes. I had never experienced anything like this.

I found a quiet spot backstage, bowed my head, and said a silent prayer. *God, use me as an instrument to bless this audience. And help Sweets to understand this is my calling. I gotta keep it real with myself.*

"Don't be nervous, son," Pop Pop whispered in my ear. How crazy was it that my seventy-year-old grandfather was watching me rap onstage for the first time. Just then, Blue rushed over to me.

"Hi, Mr. Lewis," Blue said, shaking my grandfather's hand. "Hey, Tre, lookin' good, baby! I spotted Rico Tate, so this is a great start."

When Sauce introduced me to the crowd, he gave me mad love. I thought I'd be nervous at first, but once that mic was in my hand, I knew I had to go hard.

"I decided tonight, it's take it back old school," I said, and nodded to Sauce to give me some of that beat box flava.

"Mic check one, check two. Yo, yo, yo, I do my usual, escapin' in the beat coming through my headphones, watching hood go from posh to the projects with pissy hallways and desperate souls! Martin had a dream, not deferred but heard. He took his message to the masses. They thought it was cool to shut him down but cain't no grave hold the soul of a street soldier down. So what you gotta say, lost one? Betta watch what you say before you get shook, son. Before I load up this nine with knowledge and blow you away, son. God's my only judge. Man cain't hold no grave, no grudge. . . ."

I had everyone in the room not only groovin' but thinkin' about my words and my message. My flow was better than it's ever been. Everyone in the café went bananas.

"Give it up again for my li'l homie, representin' Anacostia, givin' you flava and knowledge. Fifteen and he's a beast!" The room went crazy all over again.

When I got off the stage, I was bombarded. Blue, White-boy, Collin, and Mamie and Jade, the two girls from the studio, walked over to where my grandfather and I were standing. I gave Whiteboy a pound.

"Hey, Tre, you know we need to hook up in the studio," Mamie said.

"Cool. Talk to Blue or Collin," I said.

"You were really good," Jade said. "Girl, we'd better get back to work!" She and Mamie gave me quick hugs before rushing off.

"Great show! Mr. Lewis, this is my business partner I've been telling you about, Collin Andrews," Blue said. We all exchanged pounds. "I'll be right back. I'm going to go talk to Rico."

"Nice to meet you, sir!" Collin shook Pop Pop's hand. "Tre, you were awesome!" Collin said, giving me a fist pound.

Blue returned a few minutes later with a well-dressed guy, who extended his hand to me.

"Young Tre, this is Rico Tate," Blue said, making the special introduction.

"You were on fi-yah, li'l brotha," he said, turning to give everyone else a pound as well. "I'm late for a dinner meeting, but Blue and Collin, you got your shot next week at Club Toast. If it's a success, we'll talk about your artist. Don't forget I want a copy of that track," Rico said, making a quick exit.

"So what does that mean?" I asked eagerly.

"It means you are incredibly talented, Tre," Collin said.

"And that if our first big party is a smash, then you'll be featured at Club Toast on the regular!" Blue chimed in with enthusiasm.

"All this is fine and well, and I hate to stop this party before it starts, but we've got a long drive and school in the mornin'. Wrap it up, Tre." Pop Pop knew that Sweets was already gonna give us hell when we got home.

"Yo, I'll hit you tomorrow," Blue called out.

I thought there would be hell to pay when we got home, and there was. Sweets ripped into me for taking advantage of an "old man," and then yelled at Pop Pop for being a "stupid old man" for driving me all the way across town to some "rappin' show." I think in the end she put us both on punishment. I didn't even care. Tonight was one of those nights that goes down in history. Young Tre blew up the spot!

CHAPTER TWENTY-ONE

BLUE

Scientists say that she's the second sunshine
—Robin Thicke featuring Pharrell, "Wanna Love You Girl"

I wanted tonight to be extra special, memorable now that Blue Up had its first major party set. To top it off, it would be my first time meeting Jade's mom. I packed a picnic basket. I plugged my iPod into the car jack and made sure to download at least two hours' worth of slow jams to play. The ladies love that shit!

Jade and her mother lived in an apartment close to the DC and Silver Spring border, so she was only about a ten- or fifteen-minute drive away. That's insane. I still can't get over the fact that this dream girl has been at my same school for three years and living this close to me, and I never knew her.

I knocked on her apartment door, and her mother, a petite

woman who looked like an older, white version of Jade, answered the door.

"Um, is Jade Taylor here?" I asked.

"Come on in. You must be Blue. I'm Jade's mom."

"Nice to meet you, Mrs. Taylor," I said, reaching out to shake her hand. Damn! The palms of my hands were sopping wet with nervous sweat. I wiped them furiously on my jeans.

"Don't worry about the sweaty palms, Blue," she whispered. "It'll be our secret." She smiled. Oh, Moms had jokes. I cracked a smile as Mrs. Taylor led the way into the living room, which was a short walk down the hallway. The apartment was small but tasteful.

Her mother was dressed in a bathrobe and coughing a lot. When she turned around and offered me a seat in the chair across from where she was sitting on the couch, I could see their strong resemblance even more. Jade definitely got not only her sense of humor from her mom, but also her beauty.

"Jade will be out in a minute. So I hear you give parties?"

"Um, yes, ma'am. I want to be an entertainment mogul one day," I said. Her mother replied silently with a raised eyebrow. I figured I'd better go in with the save. "But, um, I'll probably go to law school one day too. Um, my father's a lawyer," I replied. My hands were clammy and my nervousness was on blast. "Could I please have a glass of water, Mrs. Taylor?"

"Nope, we'll be late." Jade's voice rescued me. "Hi, Blue. I'm impressed you're early. Mom, take your medicine. I'll be back before it's late," she said, leaning in to give her mom a kiss.

"You just have a good time, and you kids be careful," her mother said, walking us to the door.

When we got down to my car, I made sure to open her door and I didn't turn the music up too loud.

"Blue, are you nervous or something?" she asked.

"Why?" I quickly replied.

"Because you're not acting like you normally do. But don't get me wrong. I like this side of Blue Reynolds."

"I guess I just wondered if your mom liked me."

"What's not to like about you?" she said, kissing me as I pulled off.

I turned into the parking lot of a small upscale strip mall in front of the Blue Room restaurant. No joke. It's really called the *Blue* Room. I thought Jade might like the play on words. It's a café out in Bowie, Maryland. We had to drive about twenty minutes out to get to it, but it was worth it.

"You're not serious about the name of this place," Jade said in awe.

"Did it win me some cool points?" Jade gave me a playful shove. "The owner is a close friend of my pops. I worked here the last two summers, and during spring and winter breaks. After some major begging, and because the place is closed tonight, he let me hold the keys," I said, jumping out of the car. I grabbed the picnic basket out of the trunk, then opened her door.

"I hope you like surprises. Cover your eyes!"

When she reopened them, we were on the heated rooftop deck of the restaurant. It was tented, and white lights were strung all around the place.

"Oh, my God! It looks like there are a million stars floating around!"

"Now come over here," I said, leading her around a wall. I had a picnic blanket laid out and candles placed all around.

"Blue, this is the sweetest thing anyone's ever done for me," she said, hugging me. Jade smelled sweet, and her body fit perfectly in my arms. I wanted to tongue her down right there, I ain't playin', but I had to play it cool.

The mood was set for our late-night picnic. Soon we were chomping away on sandwiches and chips.

"To a dinner made for champions," she said, leaning over and wiping the mustard off my chin with her napkin. I was molded. Oh, girl definitely caught me grubbin' a little too hard. It was all good. I liked how her fingers felt against my face.

"Damn, my bad," I said.

"That's gonna cost you two cool points," she teased. "I have to admit this was a great idea."

"I just wanted to keep it simple. A lot of guys could take you out to eat. I wanted you to remember me," I said, turning toward her. The energy between us was magnetic.

After we finished chowing down, I hit the remote on the stereo, taking her by the hand to stand up. I'll give Chris Brown props, he made a hot one when he made his "Take You Down" joint.

Pretty soon I started to grind on Jade. Her body was perfect. Soft in all the right places, and just the right amount of booty. Babygirl was a definite ten. I began to massage her temples.

"Yeah, you got game all right, Blue Reynolds," she said with her eyes closed.

"Can I kiss you?" I asked. She nodded, and then I did, taking her in my arms and caressing her gently. We slowly kneeled down, and I slowly placed myself on top of Jade, kissing her down her neck, unbuttoning her shirt. I began to kiss around her breasts.

"Blue, please stop," she said, sitting up, her lace bra still showing. "I'm sorry. I'm not a tease. I'm not ready for this. Things just got a little carried away."

"No, I'm sorry," I said, re-buttoning her shirt. "I don't want to blow it with you."

"I'm just not trying to do anything like this right now."

"Yo, it's cool."

"So I guess the date's over?"

"Are you crazy? Yo, Jade, I'm really feelin' you. How about we just chill." She leaned back into my arms. "By the way, my father's being honored. It's a black-tie affair. Would you be my date?"

"Oh, my God, yes! I'd love to!"

"Great. And I've got the place for another couple of hours. I just wanna hold you. Is that cool?" She nodded. I turned the music up, closed my eyes, and gently stroked her hair.

CHAPTER TWENTY-TWO

COLLIN

**It's dark despite the light
Tomorrow's not in sight
—Tokio Hotel, "Black"**

"Collin, get your ass over here!" my dad shouted as soon as he saw me. He held a bank statement in the air. "What's this all about? Are you doing something you have no business doing? Do you need money that bad that you have to go behind my back? Are you on drugs?" my father demanded.

"Dad, calm down," I said, dropping my books in the foyer and walking over to him.

"I will not calm down. Tell me what this is all about!"

"I just needed the money to take care of some things. It's my money."

"Correction, it's *my* money. That account is for you to have when you go off to college," he said, tossing the statement at me.

"Dad, we have the money. How does it hurt anything?"

"Collin, it's the principle. You have no right to go behind my back. Now tell me the truth. What the hell did you need a thousand dollars for?"

"You want to know the truth? The truth is, me and Blue started a company and we needed to make a demo CD for our first artist."

"What are you talking about? That's the most ridiculous thing I've ever heard! I won't stand for you making stupid decisions and getting off track," he said, storming over to the wet bar to make himself a drink.

"Dad, it's a good plan, and we're already getting some major attention in the club world."

"Collin, what is wrong with you? Damnit, I have a reputation. I will not have my son running around town trying to be in the nightclub business. These are big shoes to fill," he said, taking a hard gulp of the Jack from his glass. He slammed his glass down on the granite bar top. The ice cubes made a hard clinking sound. "Maybe you don't get it. You're an Andrews, and the Andrews name in this town carries a lot of weight and favors."

"What are you worried about, Dad? That I'll end up like *you*?" I said, standing up to him. "Drinking too much, caring more about money and power than my family?"

"You watch your mouth!" he shouted.

"Hell, no! You've pushed everyone and everything else out

of your life, Dad! Sorry to disappoint you, but I'm the only thing left!"

"I said shut up!" And in one swift rage-filled stroke of his arm, my father whacked me across the face. I was so stunned I didn't even feel the heated sting of the impact.

"I gotta go," I said in slow, even words. My chest was heaving, but I stayed in control, calmly backing out of the room, never taking my eyes off my dad.

My Sidekick buzzed. It was Blue:

WHERE U @ FOOL? MEET ME IN THE ATRIUM
TRE'S BLOWIN' UP ON THE NET

I grabbed my backpack. As I was approached the SSH atrium area, I saw Blue. I know he was waiting on me, but today I didn't feel like dealing with him or the party, or Young Tre or anything. I kept walking as fast as I could to my car.

"Yo, C, wait up! I haven't seen you all day, and you didn't answer my text messages. Where are you going?" Blue called out, chasing after me.

"I got your messages, but I got stuff on my mind that I need to deal with," I said, walking faster. Blue was doing a slow jog to keep up with me.

"Yo, C, stop!" he said, blocking my car door. "You all right, man? I just gave you great news in my text, but you didn't reply, and you're barreling through the parking lot like a linebacker. We gotta get the PR machine in motion for the party at Club Toast. Aren't you hyped?"

"Not really. I don't really give a damn about Rico or the party!"

"What the hell is wrong with you?" he asked.

"I've just had a lot on my mind, dude. It's school, it's my dad, it's just a lot of stuff, and Blue Up caused some complications."

"This should be the best time of our lives. I got great news. I leaked Young Tre's track online, and people are going crazy!"

"You what! Blue, that's Mamie's song."

"No, it's Young Tre's song! So, we hangin' or what?" Hearing his happy-go-lucky tone made me even angrier.

"Look, dude, I'm not cool and I'm not hanging out! Don't you ever take any of this seriously? We can't do business this way!" I said, pushing past him and opening my car door.

"Collin, hold up!" He grabbed me by the arm. "I don't know what's going on, but I'm your best friend. We're boys. You gotta talk to me. You aren't acting like the same person. I thought you'd be happy about Tre's song." He held out his fist.

"I'll hit you later," I said, giving him a halfhearted fist pound.

"Collin, I'm your boy, and don't ever forget that," he said before I could close the door and drive off. "I'll fix the Mamie situation."

"When you do things like this, Blue, it defeats everything we've set out to do."

"I won't do it again. Make sure you hit me back. We've gotta heighten our promotional efforts for Club Toast. I need you."

"I'm down. Like I said, I'll hit you later."

I was going to go ballistic any minute, and for the first time I couldn't even talk to my best friend, Blue.

CHAPTER TWENTY-THREE

I'm feelin' focused man, my money on my mind
—50 Cent, "In Da Club"

A week had blown by. Thankfully, Collin got in sync and we were able to put tons of work pumping the party tonight at Club Toast in e-blasts, texts, word of mouth, the works. I know Collin like I know myself, and he just gets uptight. It's like somebody just having to walk it off. He's cool now. Okay, maybe there was still some tension between us, but, hey, we're boys. We're gonna always stick together.

I entered Cutz and Tatz with three bottles of champagne in tow. You know I had to hook my boys up with a little pre-celebratory gift. Tonight was the party at Club Toast and we had a lot to celebrate. Whiteboy started applauding.

"Well, fellas, tonight's the night. I just wanna say we are

about to seriously take over!" I said, popping the cork on my bottle of chilled champagne. Even though Collin's mind seemed to be on another planet, he followed suit, and so did Whiteboy. I wasn't going to let my boy's foul mood ruin tonight. We tapped our bottles in a toast, and I took a long swig.

"This is that good-life shit!" Whiteboy said as we let out a hearty round of laughter.

By nine o'clock, Collin and I were standing in front of Club Toast and definitely feeling like toast, *burnt* toast with a champagne buzz. Only about twenty people had showed up so far, and they were mostly the nerds at SSH. A couple of cars had driven by about five minutes earlier and kept rolling. The music was banging inside; the lights were sexy, all ready to transform what would normally be a less than exciting Club Toast into a pretty hot spot. However, the vibe was ultra wack. All those elements needed to set a party off were out of sync.

"Whassup, C? It's still early." I was jittery, but I was still hopeful for a turnout.

"Blue, you think it might be karma?"

"Yo, if you were going to be a dark cloud tonight, then maybe you shouldn't have come," I snapped. "Plus, when Young Tre gets here, we've got to make him see that Blue Up has it together."

"I'm sorry, man, but I keep thinking about Mamie. What if she's heard Young Tre's song. I don't have a good feeling. When

I say 'karma' I mean what if doing that to her makes this whole party thing backfire. Plus, we had to be crazy to think we could go up against a Georgetown Prep party," he said, leaning against the side of the club.

"Collin, I'm gonna ignore that karma comment. Leaking that song only works to Tre's best interest. No one is thinking about who produced the track. It's about him. We just gotta stay positive. It's not about failing. Maybe it's just gonna take us a minute to figure this thing out, and the next time it'll be better," I said, giving Collin a pound.

"Look, my dad is riding me about the thousand dollars I took too."

"So I'll get the money back. Just wait until our parties take off. I can't believe you're trippin' and shit. Man, you gotta know that some of this is going to be about takin' risks. If there's anything that's pissing me off right now, it's the fact that you wanna just give up! For life, man! I keep telling you that. Now, let's do this!" I held out my fist. Collin hesitated, then gave me a fist pound. "I'm gonna hit Whiteboy and see where he is," I said, reaching inside my pocket for my phone. Collin did the same. "Damn, I must've left it in the car. I'll be right back."

"Hold on!" Collin alerted me, reading from his Sidekick. "Shit, I just got a text from Whiteboy. He's been calling you for almost an hour. He said he knew some people at the Georgetown Prep party and it just got shut down! He said everyone's coming over to our party!" We high-fived.

"So let's get crackin'! GTB!" I said.

"GTB!" Collin joined the chant.

"Fo life! GTB! GTB! GTB!" I started chanting.

And get crackin' we did. . . .

Club Toast was the hottest scene in town. We had to go with the house deejay this first go-round, but he still had the party rockin'.

"Ay, yo!" I called out to my boy Collin, who was standing outside the club with at least fifteen screaming shorties in tow, some tall, some thick, but all of them wearing the skinny jeans that are *phat* in all the right places, if you know what I mean.

Homies stuntin', leaning on their gleaming whips—rimmed up, tricked-out Hondas, VW Bugs, even minivans. Hey, I'm not hatin'. Not everybody has the crazy sick ride. Me personally, I want that BMW 3 Series with the sport kit, but it's gonna take loot. At this rate, though, one day I'll have plenty of it.

"I'm lovin' it!" Collin shouted back.

"Keep it pimpin', young splashy splash, but don't get wet!" I laughed. It's all about avoiding being distracted by the pretty faces with the bangin' hot bodies. Just then Jade and Mamie rolled up.

"Whassup, Blue? Congrats on a hot turnout!" Mamie high-fived me.

"Hi, sweetie. I'm proud of you," Jade said, greeting me with a kiss.

"I'll meet you guys inside," I said, kissing her once more.

"Blue, this party is the bomb!" A dread-head slacker dude called out, throwing up the peace sign.

"Yeah, make sure you spread the word," I replied.

Thirty minutes later I was stepping behind the velvet rope into the VIP section.

"You did it!" Collin said, giving me a fist pound.

"No, *we* did it, playboy!" I replied, cracking open a Red Bull, and we toasted.

"You know you gotta let me on the ones and twos next time, Blue," Mamie said, nudging me.

"I got you. Where's your girlfriend?" I said, looking around.

"On the dance floor," she said, pointing to the center of the room. I waved at Jade, and she waved back.

Just then the crowd went crazy. All the frenzy was coming from the other side of the room.

Whiteboy had arrived! He was heading toward the VIP section, clearing the way, and with him were Young Tre and a new hot rapper named D Breezy.

"Ay, yo! What's poppin'! The spot is on fi-yah!" Whiteboy said, stepping into the VIP section, throwing both arms in the air. "This is Young Tre's night. We're breakin' him in star-style!"

"Yo, Blue, this party is crazy! You're blowin' me up online. I'm like an instant celebrity!" Young Tre beamed.

"I told you Blue Up had you covered," I said.

"Yo, this is another way to get the crowd talkin'!" Whiteboy said. "D Breezy is a big fan of Young Tre's after hearing him on the Net." Me and Collin gave him and D Breezy mad love with a round of homie pounds and high fives. Collin made a quick exit to the front door to check on the line. Whiteboy never ceased to amaze me with his hood hook ups. D Breezy was down with Lil Wayne. His surprise appearance and this big-ass crowd was going to make us the talk of the town.

"Blue, check this out," Collin said, returning to his spot next to me. He pulled a small calculator out. "I just checked with management. We have nearly four hundred kids here, at fifteen dollars a pop. We're at capacity! Next time we're definitely gonna need more space," Collin said.

"We need Rico's big money-makin' joint, Club Heat!"

"Do you realize, Blue, that if we had two parties a month at a spot like Heat, our numbers would be outta here? We could charge twenty bucks a head! Sweet!" Collin said, calculating the dollars.

"I could pay off college before I start and get me that Rover sittin' on 22s, instead of a Beemer! Sweeter!" I said, high-fiving Collin.

Jade rejoined us in the VIP, and while she and Mamie did their girl-thing, me and my boys celebrated a victory, with plenty of laughs and jokes. Collin pointed to a blonde dancing on the dance floor. Shortie was straight faded, tipsy, droppin' it like it was on fire. Me and my crew high-fived, and then the laughter died out under the bangin' Go Go track remixed with that insane new T.I. joint. I felt great. I looked around the room, and at that very moment I stood back and took in the room's energy. I smiled to myself, watching as the crowd moved in sync to the beat. Yeah, it was definitely time for me to leak the *real* Young Tre joint on the Net. Collin was just paranoid. Mamie wouldn't be able to tell it was her track.

Sometimes your instincts just tell you when your destiny's laid out before you. I can't describe it, but throwin' parties is just a means to an end. That end for me is having my own entertainment empire. I may be young, but it's about getting mine and coming up! I am the *new* American dream.

CHAPTER TWENTY-FOUR

WHITEBOY

If you can make it through the night there's a brighter day
Everything will be alright if ya hold on
—2Pac, "Dear Mama"

I was knocked out, somewhere between my second and third dream, when the phone woke me up. "Yo?" I answered groggily with mad attitude.

"Yes, is Mr. Tommy James available?" the caller asked.

"C'mon, fool, stop playin'. It's too damn early for all that. Whassup, Collin. You cool?" I said, still half asleep.

"No, Mr. James, it's Peter Mason, the associate professor of art at the Art Institute of Washington."

Oh, snap! I was jolted awake and quickly cleared my throat. "I'm very sorry, Mr. Mason. I thought you were one of my boys— I mean *friends*—playing on the phone. I mean, uh, never mind."

I cleared my throat again and tried to sound as professional as possible. "How can I help you, sir?"

"Well, this is probably more of us helping you. We think you have tremendous potential and are prepared to offer you a full scholarship to the school. Are you interested in accepting our offer, Mr. James?"

"Oh, hells, yeah! Thas whassup! Excuse me. I mean, *absolutely*!"

I must've sat in that one spot on the bed for at least fifteen minutes unable to move. I was like paralyzed. I felt like my whole life was flashing before my eyes. All the bad shit I've done, all the loses, all the hard times. But none of it mattered anymore. I only had a few people to call, but was still in shock and couldn't figure out who to tell first. Nah, I knew exactly who.

"Yo, Ms. H! Ms. H, open up. It's Tommy!"

"*Ay, dios mio.* What's going on?" she said, unlocking the door and opening it. "What is wrong, Thomas?" she said with a worried look on her face.

"I got accepted to the school!"

I thought Ms. H was gonna pass out, she was crying so hard, and then she promised to make me a celebration breakfast fit for a king. That was cool. I'd be ready to chow down after my run.

I laced up my sneaks and went out for a morning run to burn off some energy. Today I felt different from any other day. I guess that's natural when things like this happen. Nothing's ever gone down like this for me. It was like winning the lotto but even better, because I had proved that my art was worthy. I was going to be learning with and from the best.

That might seem mad corny to somebody who's always been in those situations and had education at their disposal. Blue and Collin are my boys, but they would never be able to relate to the world I came from. It's easier for me to relate to theirs, because I appreciate things differently. Being accepted into school, I feel like I can talk on the same level and take my profession to the next level.

On my way back from my run I stopped at the corner bodega to pick up some fresh flowers for Ms. H. I'd have enough time to eat, shower, and work on some new sketches before heading to work. My creative juices were flowing like crazy. Damn! Whiteboy was accepted at the prestigious Art Institute of DC.

It was all about staying focused. I don't wanna be a tattoo artist forever. I don't wanna spend the rest of my life making flyers for parties. I got dreams too, and now I can start seeing them come to fruition.

CHAPTER TWENTY-FIVE

BLUE

The world is movin' fast and I'm losin' my balance
—OutKast, "Gasoline Dreams"

"Son, let's take a ride," my pops said, leaning into the doorway of my bedroom, already dressed in his tux. I had just gotten dressed for tonight's big reception in his honor. He was strangely calm. It was a side of him I hadn't seen in a while. I mean, my pops is generally a laid-back dude, but he'd been under a lot of pressure lately with some big case and had been bringing the office home.

Maybe that's why the more I see how being a lawyer affects him, the *less* sure I am that that's something I want to do. I don't know if I want to have the life he has. I'm proud of him and I respect his hustle, but I see my path and my plight being something different.

"We're going in *my* car! Meet me in the driveway in ten minutes," he added. I figured this must be pretty serious. Pops hadn't taken his *baby* out in forever.

We stood in front of the garage, both eager to go for a spin in his wheels. As the garage door slowly ascended, I could see the tires barely peeking out from underneath the car cover.

"Oh, yeah, there she is, Blue!" My dad was practically salivating at his "pride and joy." The door was finally all the way up, and he wasted no time pulling the cover off. Oh, it was sweet all right, a candy red '74 Spitfire convertible. Dad had spent thousands refurbishing it, new engine, paint job, stereo. "Get in!" he ordered with a smile. Cool! I hopped in and we were out!

The only time my dad seems to really cool out and relax is when he's driving. That's why when I was a kid, we used to go on a lot of road trips. And this car was his true escape. He even let the top down. It was a little chilly, so he blasted the heat. Pops was totally in his element now. "Boy, when I used to take your mom out on dates in this baby—watch out now! Some things you just can't tell your kids!" He laughed.

"C'mon, Pops, the last thing I want to do is imagine you and Mom messing around. In a few more minutes, I'm gonna be sick from all the nostalgia." I frowned.

Pops pressed power on the car stereo and John Coltrane's "Lush Life" seeped through the car speakers. "Now, see, that's what *real* music is, son."

"That's aiight. I'll take Lil Wayne any day."

"Blue, where do you think all those rappers get their so-called *flows* from? They get it from jazz, gospel, the blues, man!"

"I feel you, Dad."

My pops turned up the volume. Although I had stuck my iPod in my pocket on the way out the door, I decided not to turn it on this time. I let the mellow sounds of Coltrane filter into my brain as we coasted through the lush surroundings of Rock Creek Park and on to the Rock Creek Parkway that ran alongside the river. I could understand now how driving this car helped clear his head.

When we exited onto Memorial Drive and followed the road leading into Arlington National Cemetery, I was shocked. I never in a million years imagined him bringing me to a graveyard.

"You remember? We used to drive down to Virginia in the summers to see your grandparents, Blue," he reminisced, cracking a smile.

"Yeah, I used to get so hyped when we'd load up the car and just take off," I said.

"Your grandfather was a good man, Blue. A stubborn man, but a good one," he said as we trekked our way over to a small tombstone. "You have a lot of his traits."

"Word, Dad?" I said as he placed his arm around my shoulder.

"He was the kind of man who when he set his mind on something, he meant business. He would drive my mother crazy with his stubbornness, too. One of the things he never budged on was education." I suddenly felt uncomfortable. I knew exactly where this conversation was headed.

"My father had a great deal of pride, because as a black man growing up during segregation, who eventually fought for the right to vote, and then fought in the Civil Rights Movement, getting an education was a privilege, *not* a luxury. He worked two jobs, took care of his family, and still found a way to go to Howard University. He didn't take it lightly, and neither do I. He didn't have a lot of money, but he had dreams that his children and their children would always have education to fall back on."

"Dad, I understand all that, but I feel like you don't understand my dreams!"

"Blue, you know I've always been in your corner and support you on every front. But let me tell you something about dreams. Dreams can suffocate you if you don't act on them correctly. Think about that, son. That was my point in coming out here today."

"Okay, Dad," I said, looking down at my grandfather's headstone.

"The award I'm getting tonight from my alma mater is one of the biggest awards of my career. I just wish my father was here to see this. I mean, I get accolades from my colleagues at the big firms and even in the *Washington Post*, but nothing compares to this. See, son, it's really about your legacy. What legacy will you leave behind?

"I just want you to remember that life isn't a party. You can't compare a good time at a club to the accomplishments of lawyers like Thurgood Marshall! Now, get your mind right, son. Get your priorities in order and don't disappoint men like your grandfather. I'm looking forward to when you proudly follow in my footsteps!" Dad gave me a hearty pat on the back and then a rowdy you're-my-son-and-my-homie pound. "Let's go. We're gonna be late!"

On the ride home we were both silent. I just sat in the passenger seat wishing that I was somewhere else. My dad didn't deserve for me to disappoint him, but I have to be true to myself, don't I? I've been reading a lot, and I understand this music game. It doesn't even take a college degree to run a record company. What it takes is drive and hands-on experience.

Bottom line, I've got some other plans when it comes to *my* future. I mean, what if I don't necessarily want to become a lawyer like him? Hey, it's about keeping your options open, right? If somethin' pops off sooner as opposed to later, then I'm tryin' to rock with it. You've gotta get in to fit in, right? But college versus no college period is a whole *other* level of drama I know I'll have to deal with later with the parentals.

At the gala reception my dad was beaming with pride and so was I as I watched him glide through the posh ballroom at the Four Seasons in Georgetown with his tux on, my mom in her long gown by his side. Pops was a smooth dude, I had to give it to him. Tonight was his night, and everyone was talking about the great achievements of Attorney David Langston Reynolds.

Jade was by my side, and that was the second-best thing of the night. She looked hot in a black fitted cocktail dress. No lie, my girl was turning me on big-time. It was hard for me to concentrate while the president of Howard University was speaking about my father's accomplishments. I licked my lips and mouthed, *I want you*. Jade kicked me lightly under the table.

When my dad was called up to the stage to get the Presidential Alumni Award of Merit, my mother couldn't hold back and burst into an emotional puddle of tears. The biggest shock came, though, when my father asked me to stand.

"I want to introduce everyone in this room to my son, Blue Reynolds. He's looking to attend Howard when he graduates, and keep the Reynolds legal legacy alive!" The room exploded with applause. At that point I just wanted the night to be over.

After dinner they cleared an area for dancing. One of my father's former classmates swooped in on me like a hawk. "Blue, if you're anything like your dad, you're gonna make one hell of an attorney. What type of law do you want to practice?"

"I'm not sure, sir, maybe entertainment," I answered, semi-distracted by my buzzing Sidekick.

"You're David's son, right?" Another overly friendly person

bum-rushed me. "Your father is quite a trailblazer." I was losing my patience with these people.

"Oh, this must be your lovely girlfriend. She's beautiful," someone else said, passing me a business card.

"Can you excuse me," I said, cutting the person off. "Come on, Jade," I said, pulling her out of the room.

"What's going on? I was having a great time."

"I just needed some air." I suddenly felt sick from all the superficial people in the room, talking about alma maters, summer houses, and this firm versus that firm. I had had enough. This life was for my dad, but probably not for me.

"Part of me wants to carry the Reynolds legal legacy into the next generation. The other part wants to make my own legacy. However, what's crystal clear is that I can't let Blue Up go."

"Then don't, Blue. Follow your heart," Jade said, touching the side of my face.

"Jade, if I do this thing right, my dreams to one day parlay all the hard work Collin and I are going to put into Blue Up into an empire *will* come true. It's all about using one situation to make another one better!"

"But first you have to graduate high school. I guess for me, not going to college isn't an option."

"Unfortunately, I'm not so sure my parents will understand my plan. I'm eight months from turning eighteen. Basically, I'm a grown man and I'm at a place in my life where I have to start making my own decisions. I just hope that when the time comes, my dad will understand."

"Well, what he won't understand is you leaving. This is a pretty special night for him." Jade kissed me.

"You're incredible, and you're right." I took her hand and led her back inside the party.

CHAPTER TWENTY-SIX

Don't tell me you're sorry 'cause you're not
—Rihanna, "Take a Bow"

"Girl, the gala was incredible. I felt like a princess standing next to Blue. And guess what Blue purchased for me?" I said, dangling a bag from Bebe in the air, walking toward Mamie, who was busying herself in the break room. "How cute is this?" I reached in the bag and pulled out a hot pink strapless satin dress. "I think I'm going to wear it to Blue's next party."

"Great! Just what I don't need," Mamie muttered under her breath, stomping past me to the mirror on the other side of the room.

"What's up with the stank hater attitude, chickie?" I teased, putting my hands on my hips.

"You know what? Screw you and yo man Blue!" She

whipped around and faced me like she was ready to fight.

"What the hell is all this about, Mamie!"

"Ask your boyfriend!" she said, yanking her apron from a nearby chair.

"Ask him what?"

"Ask him does it feel good being a thief!" She charged past me.

"Mamie, what are you talking about? Talk to me!" I shouted.

"Your man stole one of my tracks and used it for Young Tre. It's all over MySpace and I didn't get any credit. As a matter of fact, it says produced by Blue Reynolds. Yeah, he got me real good, but never again."

"I'm sorry, Mamie. I'm sure there's a good explanation."

"Are you sayin' I'm a liar?" She frowned, stepping close to my face. "After all we've been through together, some Negro can just come all up in your life, get you open with a few nice words and a freakin' dress?" she asked, snatching the dress out of my hands and throwing it across the room. Tears streamed down my face. "I don't give a damn about your tears. I never should've trusted you. You ain't my friend. Jade is about Jade getting hers. So you know what? Mamie is about to be about hers, too. Thanks for lookin' out!"

I collapsed into a nearby chair and cried until my face hurt. Then I picked my dress up off the floor and gathered my purse and tote bag, and left out the back door. As far as I was concerned they could fire me. I had just lost my best friend.

By the time I stepped off the Metro, my face was streaked with a mixture of mascara and tears. Cutz and Tatz was just up ahead, and I could see Blue's mom's car parked out front. When I reached the shop's door, it felt like fire was surging through my veins.

"How could you do that to her! How could you steal from my friend?" I shouted. Everyone in the shop was staring at me, but I didn't give two shits.

"Jade, baby, chill! Let's talk about this outside," Blue said nervously, looking around as he put his arm around me and led me back outside. His stupid friend Whiteboy was standing with his mouth open in shock.

"No, let's not talk about this!" I said, pulling away from him. "You did my girl dirty!"

"I can explain—"

"Don't explain shit!" I said, cutting him off. "I don't have my best friend anymore because of you. I thought you were different. I have no idea who you are. The Blue Reynolds I thought I was falling in love with doesn't do shit like this." I pulled the Bebe bag out of my tote and handed it to him. I didn't need him or his gifts. "I thought you were at least honest," I said, turning away from him. When I realized a crowd had gathered in the window of the shop, I felt completely embarrassed. "I gotta go!"

"Let me talk to you! Let me give you a ride, Jade!" he called out. I gave him the hand. I just wanted to get as far away from Blue Reynolds as I could.

CHAPTER TWENTY-SEVEN

Man, I got summer hatin' on me 'cause I'm hotter than the sun
Got spring hatin' on me 'cause I ain't never sprung
—Lil Wayne, "Mr. Carter"

I sent three urgent messages to Collin:

I'VE GOT GOOD NEWS & BAD NEWS

MEET ME OUTSIDE CLUB HEAT IN AN HOUR

@ RICO TATE'S OFFICE

By the time Collin pulled up in front of Club Heat, I'd worn a groove in the cement pavement.

"What's the emergency, Blue? I was in a study group, and you were blowing me up!"

"Do you want to hear the good news or the bad news first?"

"Your pick, and why did you have me meet you here?" he asked. Wrinkles formed across his forehead.

"Great question. First off, Rico was blown away by the report back on the party at Club Toast. He wants to meet with us tonight."

"Okay, that's great. Now, what's the second part?"

"The not-so-great incident of the day is that we have a problem with Mamie."

"You never fixed things and she found out about the song, didn't she?" Collin blew out a frustrated breath.

"I messed up bad, C, and stuff is falling apart. You were right. My karma is screwed," I said, pacing back and forth again. "Mamie found out about Young Tre's song, she went to Jade, Jade fronted me at Cutz and Tatz, and there was a big blowup. Now they aren't friends anymore, we don't have Mamie, and I've lost my girl. I also wasn't completely honest about something else."

"Damn, there's more? Jeez!"

"Look, I don't have that signed contract from Young Tre."

"Are you serious? Blue, we're screwed all the way around."

"I gotta fix things," I said.

"You're damned right! I haven't even been speaking to my father as a result of my decision to do Blue Up. I'm jeopardizing my future and making sacrifices for what we're trying to do, and then you go and do things behind my back! Not cool. Not cool at all, Blue."

"I'm sorry, but we gotta meet with Rico, so you can't bail on me now."

"Blue and Collin, Mr. Tate will see you now." Rico's secretary peeked out the large front doors of the club and motioned for us to come inside.

"You're right. We're too deep into this thing. But don't apologize to me. You have to apologize to Mamie. Kiss her ass, buy her dinner, whatever. You're the master schmoozer," Collin sarcastically commented under his breath as we entered Club Heat.

Rico's secretary led the way into Rico Tate's opulent office in the back of the massive Club Heat in midtown DC. Blue and I looked at each other and nodded in agreement. Impressive!

"Dude, my palms are sweaty and clammy again. This guy always freaks me out," Collin said under his breath.

"I got this!"

"Yeah, right, just like you had Mamie and Tre," Collin said, rolling his shoulders to release the stress I had just hit him with.

Rico entered and seemed in a hurry. "I don't have much time, but thanks for stopping by," he said, sitting on the edge of his large mahogany desk. "I hear the party had a great turnout and I'd like to try you guys out again at the end of the month. But this time I need something bigger. I need a performance, like the one from that kid, Young Tre. That song is getting heat, and even the deejays on the radio on WKYS are talking about it."

"Well, sir, we'll have to check on—"

"No problem," I said, cutting Collin off. He shot me a steely look.

"Yeah, Blue will get back to you on that front. I guess my question has more to do with stepping up our dealings with you. We turned around your deadest night at Club Toast. Perhaps we could work out a percentage more in the territory of sixty-forty for the next party," Collin proposed.

"Maybe Club Heat is even an option," I added.

"Unbelievable! One party doesn't convince me to give you Club Heat. This is prime nightlife entertainment real estate here. Now, what I will do is let you take your little rapper down to WKYS and promote his appearance. You'd have to be at the station tomorrow at five o'clock on DJ Quicksilver's show. That is, if you still want Club Toast." He chuckled. "I've got a pressing engagement, so you'll have to excuse me. I can't believe you said sixty-forty. You guys are really entertaining. You might want to take this little show on the road. I suggest you take seventy-thirty at Club Toast before all bets are off."

We were dismissed, and Collin was even more pissed.

"Blue, you never cease to amaze me!" Collin was emphatic, jumping in his car and starting the engine. He powered his window down. "It's almost becoming comical how that hole we're in keeps getting deeper and deeper," he said, shaking his head.

"Look, C, I'll get the deal signed. I can deliver the kid. And I'll make things straight with Mamie."

"You'd better, because we have to be at that radio station tomorrow."

"I need to get to Jade first, and then we can find Mamie."

"Mamie's usually at one of two places, the Spot or Busboys."

When we pulled up in front of Busboys, I saw Jade through the café's large windows. Collin waited in the car while I went inside. I figured if I went to her job, she'd have to be somewhat restrained. It was the safest bet. I made a smooth entrance and went directly to the back of the room near the kitchen and restroom areas. I figured I'd wait until she either picked up an order or had to go to the ladies' room.

"Jade, please!" I said, blocking her path.

"Don't come near me," she said through gritted teeth. I had to block her in a corner to keep her from getting away.

"Jade, all I'm asking is for you to hear me out."

"I can't believe this. I cannot make a scene at my job."

"I'll leave as soon as I finish explaining."

"What are you, a stalker or something? I've gotten all ten thousand of your texts. Obviously, you don't get hints, so I'll be clear. Stop calling, stop texting, stop coming to my job!"

"All I want is two minutes," I said, staring her in the eyes.

"Fine. You have two minutes before I start screaming."

"I was wrong stealing Mamie's track. I was desperate, but more importantly, my ego got in the way."

"What? You just didn't want to see a sista come up or something?" she said, folding her arms.

"I wanted to look like the superhero. I realize that's not how I want to build my career. I got caught up, and now not only is Blue Up messed up, but so are all my relationships. I'm on the verge of losing my best friend, and I've lost the woman I love." I swallowed hard. "Yes, I realize that I love you and you're more important to me than parties and all that stuff. I want Blue Up to blow up, but I want it to blow up the right way, and I want somebody to have my back and hold me down, or it isn't worth it. I want to make things right with your girl and I *need* to make things right with you."

"Blue, I don't know," she said, fighting back tears. "I'm more concerned about Mamie than I am you and me. She won't talk to me and hasn't been to work or school. I know she's been at that club, because I called."

"I meant what I said. I love you. I know you're the one for me. Please help me clear things up with Mamie."

"You put me in the middle of things. I didn't even know what was going on. You can't use people like that. People have feelings."

"I understand that now."

"I'm getting off early tonight. So just wait for me outside, please." Jade smoothed down her hair and apron and collected herself. "I'm doing this for Mamie, not for you!"

I was just happy Jade didn't cut me off completely. I know

I have a lot to make right between us, and even with Collin and Mamie. It may sound bad, but maybe I needed things to happen like this so I could fully understand how lucky I really am. And if by some miracle everything gets back on track, I won't ever sell out the people I care about again, and that's real talk.

"IT'S ALL MESSED UP NOW."

CHAPTER TWENTY-EIGHT

MAMIE

Diva is a female version of a hustla
—Beyoncé, "Diva"

Tonight the owner of the Spot didn't need a filler or a backup deejay. I just didn't want to be at my aunt's house. It was better that way. At some point, she's going to really kick me out and I'll have to figure out my next move. I've had school on my mind too. What do I do if this deejay thing doesn't work out? Aunt Deb is right. I can't really put that on a résumé. I just feel like giving up. I lost my best friend over some straight BS.

Oh, hells no! I looked up, and Jade and her two sorry comrades were walking in the club. "Well, if it isn't the traitor." I rolled my eyes. "Go ahead, girl. I'm not gonna trip. I guess that's how you roll!" I grabbed my purse.

"Mae, stop!" Jade said, blocking my path. "I came here

because I've been miserable. You are as close as a sister to me, and I can't lose you." Jade started to cry.

"You know you get me with those tears," I said, fighting back my own. I hugged her.

"I'm sorry. I didn't know anything about the track, and I broke up with Blue. I let him and Collin come with me tonight because they owed you a face-to-face apology. But regardless of what happens with you and them, I need you. You're my sister, and I would never ever hurt you." By this time Jade had a full-fledged cry on.

"Chickie, you gotta stop cryin'. We're in the club," I said, making her laugh between the tears. "Look, I was angry at Blue and Collin so I took it out on you. That's the story of my life. I lash out at anything that hurts." I put my arm around her shoulder.

"Mamie, I have to apologize too," Collin said, stepping closer to me. "I honestly didn't know what Blue had done, but when I found out, I didn't stop him, so that makes me just as guilty. I tried texting you, but you never replied."

"And?"

"And your friendship means a lot to me."

"Look, I'm the one who created this whole mess," Blue said as I gave him the hand and turned to walk back to my seat. "I was an asshole. I was so desperate to blow up I didn't care who I hurt in the process," he continued.

"Blue, guys like you kill me. You've got it all with your cars, college funds, all that crap. Me, I've been strugglin' on the grind my whole life. I can only depend on me, nobody else. So I'm never going to sacrifice my integrity for anybody. I'll never let my music be stolen again. Just like my beats will never be bartered with booty! It might take me a little bit longer to get to the top, but I'mma get there the respectable way. I gotta go. That is, if you're done!" I folded my arms across my chest as if to dare him to say the wrong thing.

"Mamie, again, I'm sorry, and I will fix everything if you give me a chance. I want to do business the right way with you. I'll make sure the song is never used again, but this is bigger than the song. Just please reconsider." He extended his hand. I turned my nose up at him and went to sit down.

"C'mon, Mae. They're trying," Jade said, sitting down next to me.

"I'm not that easy, Jade! I've got to stand up for myself this time. I forgive you, but I just can't let them off the hook."

"Mae, don't sacrifice your dream because your ego is bruised. You'll be no different than Blue. We're all young, and we're gonna make mistakes. I think they want to make things right. Just think about it." Jade motioned for the two Stooges to leave, then hugged me again. I was happy to have my girl back, but didn't give a damn about Blue or Collin.

CHAPTER TWENTY-NINE

It's my destiny, to make history
—LL Cool J, "The G.O.A.T."

Collin and I had barely said ten words to each other while we waited in the lobby of 93.9 WKYS for Tre to come back from the bathroom. Both of us were frustrated about the situation.

"He'd better not get on the air without this contract signed," Collin mumbled.

"Look, I said I was gonna get his signature. I can't just bum-rush him, though."

When Tre returned, Collin and I abruptly ended our conversation.

"Yo, this is crazy. This is one of the biggest days of my life and what should be the biggest day for Blue Up, and y'all are actin' like it's a funeral. What's the real deal? I'm not diggin' this vibe, and as an artist I can't perform the way I need to under these conditions. Somebody speak the truth," Tre said, looking at both me and Collin.

"Go ahead, Blue, you do the honors," Collin snapped.

"Listen, Tre, I haven't handled some things the right way. I need your signature on that contract, and I also need to confess something about that track we recorded for your demo. I didn't produce it. Actually, Mamie, my girl's friend—well, ex-girl's friend—produced it."

"You mean honey from the studio who's the deejay?" Tre asked. "Wow, that explains the message I got from her on my Facebook page. She said that was her track, but I didn't believe her. Is that how Blue Up gets down?"

"No, it's not, Tre," Collin said, stepping in. "But sometimes in business you make mistakes and you don't use the best judgment. *We* realized what we did wrong and we want to try to fix things now. We all have a lot at stake here." I couldn't believe that despite everything I had messed up, Collin was still showing me that he was down.

Just then the show's producer motioned for us to head into the studio. Once we were in the booth, DJ Quicksilver's assistant passed us each a set of headphones.

"We only have five minutes for y'all to do your thing. Rico Tate said to put you on, so get it poppin'," DJ Quicksilver said.

When the red ON AIR light came on, I knew I had to make this moment as meaningful as possible.

"Whassup, DC. We got some folks in the house that are makin' some serious noise. I heard this kid online, and I was blown away. Young Tre, holla at ya peoples," DJ Quicksilver said.

"Yo, I just wanna say thanks to God, to my grandma and grandfather for raisin' me right, and to Anacostia for holdin' me down. This is for my peoples in the struggle and to all my peoples at Duke Ellington School of the Arts. A check it, check it, check it out. *You still talkin' 'bout cars, clothes, and dough. I'm talkin' 'bout whatchu know. Knowledge is my dough. Spend that paper wisely, yo. Like Wayne say, blind eyes could look at me and still see the truth. Young Tre's the name, and I got nothin' left to say!*"

"That's what I'm talkin' about. Young Tre's fifteen and puttin' it down. So I just wanna let y'all know he's gonna be performing at Club Toast at the end of the month, and that's being brought to you by Blue Up Productions. They're on the come up!" DJ Quicksilver motioned to me to get on the mic.

"Yeah, yeah, we're doin' big things and redefining entertainment for the under twenty-one crowd, but these are the next generation of movers and shakers. It's all about that upscale, young, flashy, and classy crowd! But I wanna give a quick shout-out!"

"We runnin' out of time, but do ya thang!" DJ Quicksilver joked.

"A lot of blood, sweat, and tears have gone into Blue Up, and our paper chase is definitely strong. My partner, Collin, holds me down, but also, that song that's heating up all over wasn't produced by me. It was produced by DJ Ill Mama. She's one of the dopest deejays on the ones and twos, and one of the dopest new, hot producers around. So we hope Blue Up can do some big things with her. And a shout-out to my girl, Jade."

"Okay, okay, and yo mama and daddy, too. Blue took up all the time, but it's all good. Don't forget to check out their next joint. I have a feelin' they're gonna be takin' this game to another level."

I felt great after the show. And no matter what happened with Tre's contract, Mamie, or even Rico Tate, I felt like I had done the right thing.

"That was great what you did in there, Blue," Collin said, giving me a fist pound.

"Yo, that was a big look. And, um, I actually have something for you guys." Tre reached into his backpack and pulled out a signed copy of the agreement. "I had it, but I wasn't sure about giving it to you. But what you did in there let me know that Blue Up got my back. And whatever I need to do to help you get Ill Mama, I'm down. I definitely think me and her could do some insane music together."

Just then my Sidekick buzzed. It was Jade:

THANK U FOR THE SHOUT OUT
& U DID THE RIGHT THING
@ WORK GOTTA GO

I smiled. It buzzed again. It was from Rico Tate. "Hold on. Rico just sent me a message!" I read it out loud.

U DID URE THING LET'S MAKE CLUB HEAT HAPPEN INSTEAD OF TOAST TOP FLOOR ONLY,
60/40 SPLIT GET THAT FEMALE DJ

"Sweet!" Collin said, giving me a high five.

"Dope! I'm down with Blue Up. Let's do this!" Young Tre was in.

"I got an idea, and at this point we don't have anything to lose, do we?" Collin said. I nodded. I knew exactly what move he wanted to make.

By the time we got to Busboys and Poets, Jade and Mamie were getting off. Me, Collin, and Young Tre were leaning against Collin's car in front.

"Oh, hells no. Now it's the Three Stooges!" Mamie stopped and turned to Jade, who was standing next to her.

"They look pitiful, though, Mae," Jade said, and giggled.

"Mamie, I'm truly sorry, and you deserve all your props."

"Nice try putting me on blast on the radio. I'll give you a half a point for effort," Mamie said, rolling her eyes.

"Mamie, we need you. Club Heat is going to happen, but it won't be the same without you," Collin pleaded.

"On the real, I think it took mad courage for Blue to correct his mistake. I wanna work with you, and I'd love to get on that stage at Club Heat and rock the house with that track." Thank God for Tre's words. He made Mamie's eyes light up. She whispered in Jade's ear.

"Well, on behalf of my client, I'll say that she's willing to give Blue Up a try, but she wants something in writing that states she's the official Blue Up Productions deejay."

I stepped up to Mamie and extended my hand. "Tell your client she has a deal!" I was nervous, because for a few seconds Mamie left me hanging, but then she shook my hand. Collin rushed in and gave her a big-ass hug, and I couldn't take my eyes off Jade.

"I know I've done more things wrong than right, but I need you. I love you, Jade."

"I love you too, Blue!"

I took Jade in my arms and held her tightly like I was hanging on for dear life.

So I had my girl, my boy, and a winning duo of talent. Club Heat was about to be on!

CHAPTER THIRTY

COLLIN

If I don't do nothin' I'mma ball
I'm countin' all day like the clock on the wall
—Playaz Circle featuring Lil Wayne, "Duffle Bag Boy"

I was just about to hit the lights after a long day and an even longer, but nonetheless great, night when I heard a knock at my bedroom door.

"Collin, it's your dad. Can I talk to you for a minute?"

I was stuck between shocked and confused by my father's calm tone and effort as I opened the door.

"Sure. Come on in."

"I wanted to apologize for hitting you the other day," my father said, lowering his eyes. For the first time since I was a kid I saw and felt a sense of humanity in him. He was actually sincere. "Sometimes I just don't think you realize the level of dedication and work it takes to succeed."

"Dad, I do. No one pushes me harder than I do. It hurts that you don't see the things I do."

"Collin, mothers are there to coddle their kids. My job is to prepare you. Is that so wrong?"

"No, Dad, but you treat me like I'm some kind of stranger. I'm your son! Your son! Nothing I can do is ever good enough for you. No matter how hard I study, or how many A's I get, or how many honors I receive!"

"Son, the past few years have been tough. I don't want to lose anyone else I love."

I looked up at my father and watched his eyes puddle up. We never talked about anything from the past. Maybe tonight wasn't the night to start.

I collapsed in a nearby chair, and my father did something he hadn't done in years. He walked over and hugged me. I wasn't sure what all this meant or what the next steps were. The only thing I knew for sure was that my father and I were both holding too much anger inside.

"Listen, Collin, I have dinner scheduled with the president of Georgetown and several other alums from Wall Street and politics on the twenty-third. It'll be great for you, and a great way for us to start doing some things together."

"I'd love to, but Blue and I have a big party on the twenty-third," I said. My father stood up erect and tilted his head to the side.

"Then you have to make a choice, don't you? But I expect it to be the smart one."

My father left me sitting with one of the heaviest decisions I've ever had to make. What the hell was I going to do?

I needed to talk to Blue. I had a dilemma. The party was important, but so was that dinner my father had planned. I shot a quick text off to Blue, asking him to meet me in the library.

I checked my watch, and he was running ten minutes behind. I looked over the railing and saw him trekking through the lower level with his iPod on. I fired off a quick text:

UPSTAIRS—C

He still didn't see me until I waved him over to the booth I was sitting in.

"One more day, playboy!" Blue said, greeting me with our signature fist pound.

"I've gotta talk to you. I may not be able to be at the party tomorrow."

"What? Dude, you have to be there. What's going on? I see the stress all over your face."

"Things have been weird for a while between me and my dad. Basically, bad. I got my SAT scores and got a 2300, but that still wasn't good enough for him. Then he pulled some major strings to get me into Georgetown's prestigious summer program."

"I'm sorry. I didn't hear a problem. That's incredible, pimpin'!" Blue reached over and gave me a high five.

"The problem is that I can't please my father, and that's a hard pill to swallow. So, I'm thinking about rejecting the invitation to go to Georgetown." I grabbed my head with my hands.

"Why, dude? That's crazy! Georgetown is all you think about. That program is your way in," Blue said.

"Look, it's either got to be my father's way or my way. It can't be both. Why do the program if I'll have to be under scrutiny the whole time."

"C, let all that go. That's just nerves. Your pops is putting his issues on you. You know in your heart what the right decision is. You're just getting cold feet. Shake it off. The party's gonna set the tone from here on out and make us an instant household name. That's what all this has been for! Sometimes in life you gotta go for the gut instinct, roll the dice. I gotta bounce! Tomorrow!"

To Blue it's as simple as going with your gut. Problem is, I don't know what my gut is saying. My tat was supposed to be my motivation to live my life for me, but that doesn't seem to be working.

CHAPTER THIRTY-ONE

BLUE

And party and bullshit . . .
—Notorious B.I.G., "Party and Bullshit"

The party hadn't even started yet and the mob outside Club Heat was growing bigger and bigger, with people lining up to get into the hottest eighteen and under joint the DC metro area had ever seen. WKYS, Facebook, and MySpace were buzzing about Young Tre and DJ Ill Mama. Blue Up was all people were talking about. There were six bouncers dressed in black suits stationed outside the club. I spotted Jade and Mamie. "Jade! Jade!" I motioned for the bouncers to clear the way. They parted the crowd like the Red Sea.

"It's hectic," I said, kissing her on the lips. "I'll meet you guys in VIP. Mamie, you and Young Tre are on at eleven. After giving Jade another kiss, I quickly returned to the mayhem. I got behind the velvet rope just in time before the crowd started pushing and shoving. I had to guard the most valuable item of the night—the guest list. Everyone was pressed to get inside. I spotted Whiteboy and Young Tre and motioned for the bouncers to bring them through too.

"Get used to it, baby! This is all for you. You about to blow up like nitro, kid!" I told Tre as we gave each other a fist pound.

"Yo, where's Collin?" Whiteboy asked.

"I don't know." I gave a worried expression.

"B, he'll be here. I'd better get Tre inside before he takes all my honey action!"

"You'd better leave these young girls alone before you catch a case!" I joked.

"Oh, damn, here comes my ex, Nikki," Whiteboy said, inconspicuously pointing to a brown-skinned shorty who looked like Gabrielle Union. She walked over and pulled her Gucci shades off. "Whassup, Blue? Oh, you don't know nobody, Whiteboy?"

"My bad, Nikki!" Whiteboy said, doing a doubletake before leaning in and giving Nikki a kiss on her cheek. Nikki waved at someone else and then made her way over to the other side of the crowd.

"I was hoping I didn't run into her, but groupies need love too, right? Yo, she been beggin' me to hit it since we broke up. Nikki's fine as hell, but I ain't got time to get caught up in that drama."

"You are a fool!" I said.

"Okay, I'm out for real. I'll be up in VIP." Whiteboy dashed off. I took one last look at the crowd. Collin still wasn't in sight. Oh, well, I had to hold it down for both of us. Tonight Blue Reynolds was taking the art of partying to the next level.

When I walked inside, I was led by one of the bouncers to the elevator that would take me to the club's second floor. When the doors opened, I could see the dance floor was covered with bodies. It was like the number of beautiful people had quadrupled, moving the party to Club Heat. I think every bad chick from Silver Spring to Virginia called her fine-ass cousin and then her fine-ass friend and made them come with her. But I was cool on all that, actually.

For the first time ever Blue Reynolds was representin' for the fellas on lockdown. Jade had me open. I know that's not cool to say, but damn, look at her. Jade was dancing sexily in VIP. The manager of Heat interrupted my daydream.

"Dude, we're almost at capacity. We gotta stop lettin' fools in," he said, looking around nervously.

"But we're making a shitload of money. The show doesn't even start till eleven. That's another hour. Let's wait another fifteen to twenty minutes. And can you let me know when my partner, Collin Andrews, gets here? I'll be in VIP."

"Cool. Then we're on shutdown mode," he said, before heading back down to the front of the club.

When I walked into VIP, I felt like I was getting the presidential treatment. Everyone was giving me pounds and pats on the back for such a hot party.

"Yo, have you heard from C yet?" Whiteboy asked.

"No, but something just don't seem right. He hasn't returned any of my text messages."

"You know your boy. He's probably chillin'. He'll be here soon. He might already be here and we just haven't seen him yet. I'm gonna go and check the front once more before the show starts." I noticed Whiteboy's facial expression drop.

"Hey, you good? You seem jumpy all of a sudden."

"Yeah, yeah. I just thought I saw that fool who rolled up on me in front of the shop that night. Don't pay any attention to me. I'm gonna go look for C," Whiteboy said, darting off, but not before scanning the direction he was looking in one more time.

I was just about to head to the dance floor when I spotted Collin on the other side of the club.

"A-yo, C!" I waved him over. "I thought you weren't gonna show."

"I got dressed and got halfway to a really big dinner with my dad and his Georgetown colleagues, but this is where my heart is."

"So let's do this!" I said, giving him a hearty fist pound.

After about an hour, Mamie took the stage, and all the guys and girls in the crowd went wild. The guys wanted her and the girls wanted to *be* her. I slid in the booth behind Jade, but not before pulling her hair back and kissing her neck. Damn, I wanted her. Tonight wasn't the place or time to talk, but now that we were back together, a brotha wanted to know just how long she was gonna make me wait.

"Whassup, party people. I'm your girl DJ Ill Mama on the ones and twos, and in just a little bit we're gonna bring out my boy Young Tre!" The crowd went wild. "But first let's keep it young, flashy, and classy!" Mamie said, spinning in some classic Mary J, "Real Love." I grabbed Jade's hand and pulled her closer. Nikki managed to make her way into VIP and was droppin' it like it was hot all over Whiteboy. Collin was keepin' it smooth and simple sipping on a Red Bull. An Asian babe was trying her best to get with him.

"I think your boy likes Mamie," Jade whispered in my ear.

"Nah, they're just friends," I said.

"Whatever," she said, reaching for her buzzing phone.

"No, tonight it's all about me and you," I said, leaning in to kiss her.

A few minutes after eleven I took the stage and grabbed the mic. "Give it up for Ill Mama. When I say Blue, you say Light! Blue!"

"Light!" the crowd cheered.

"If anybody wants to hear that hot joint by Young Tre and Ill Mama, let me hear you say ho!"

Mamie kicked it off with the base line from that classic Biggie Smalls, "Give Me One More Chance." Each time she switched the record, she came with something even hotter— Slick Rick, T.I., Weezy, Jay-Z. Then she hit the ladies with some Beyoncé. Tre grabbed the mic and started to rip it!

"This is insane!" Collin said.

"I don't know how he got out of the house tonight, and I'm not asking," I said.

"Yeah, but tonight is just the beginning. His star has officially launched," Collin said, passing a round of Red Bulls around.

"To gettin' mine and yours! Holla!" Jade toasted before grabbing her phone. "Something's wrong." She frowned. "I gotta go call home."

"I'll go with you," I said.

"No, it might take a while, and you need to stay here," she said, kissing me and exiting VIP.

"To the ultimate come up!" I interjected, nodding at Collin.

Just when Tre and Mamie were about to go into another song, and I thought the night was too good to be true, I noticed what appeared to be a scuffle in the back of the room.

"Dude, what's going on?" Collin shouted loudly in my ear.

"Hi, Blue. I've heard a lot about you." An exotic-looking girl extended her hand. "I'm Mischa," she said, climbing into my booth and onto me.

"I saw security go over there. I'm sure it's fine," I said to Collin, trying to peel the new stranger, Mischa, off of me. She was grinding and gyrating her body against me. "Look, this isn't cool!" I said, trying not to be rude.

"Um, excuse you." Jade cut her eye at Mischa. "Blue, what the hell is going on!" Jade grabbed her purse.

"I don't even know this chick!" I said, pushing the girl off me one last time.

"I've gotta go. No one's answering at home and I have a bad feeling." She gave me the hand. "I'm sorry. I got too much going on in my life for drama, Blue." Jade stormed off and slipped through the crowd so fast that I couldn't see her.

Then, just when I thought the night couldn't get any more screwed, that small scuffle broke into a major ruckus.

"Dude! Oh, shit, it's Whiteboy!" Collin said, grabbing me by the arm. We jumped over thrown chairs and bar stools and found ourselves in the middle of the entire fight.

"Go get your preppy, punk-ass boys now!" Lopez shouted.

"I don't know nothin' about you and Rook's—" Before Whiteboy could get his sentence out, Lopez punched him in the face. He stumbled to the floor. I tried to reach for Whiteboy, but he rammed headfirst into Lopez's stomach, knocking him on his back. Whiteboy proceeded to give him a first-class hood beat-down.

By this time other partygoers had jumped in on the action and everybody was fighting. There were so many people even the bouncers had trouble stopping the fight. A melee exploded. But when somebody heard the word "police," people started to scatter. Whiteboy also took off running to keep from getting locked up.

After the crowd cleared out and the lights were on, I looked at Collin, and his head was buried in his hands. I'd lost my girl for sure this time, the club was practically destroyed, and all the money we made would have to be turned over to Rico Tate's people for the damages. I was furious at Whiteboy.

Two hours later we were sitting in my driveway.

"I've been texting Jade like crazy, but she won't respond or answer my calls."

I fired off three messages back-to-back:

IT'S ME PLS CALL ME BACK

ARE U OK I'M WORRIED

I LOVE YOU J I GOT CAUGHT UP

"She's not home, and I don't know where to begin looking for her. My Sidekick finally buzzed. It was from Jade:

MOMS IN HOSPITAL
PLS DON'T CALL ANYMORE

"Damn! She doesn't want to talk to me and her mom is sick!" I was stressed.

"Yeah, well, I hear you, but I'm trying to track down White-boy while you're runnin' drama," Collin said with an attitude. "We gotta talk, Blue. This party thing got scary tonight."

"Yeah, but we'll make a deal with Rico and fix it!"

"Fix it? For once you gotta be realistic. We're going to owe this guy so much money we won't have to worry about whether to go to college or not. It won't be an option," Collin said, turning to me.

"I know we can work it out. Things just got out of hand."

"No, Whiteboy got outta hand!" Collin angrily shouted. "But he's definitely not the only person outta hand."

"What the hell are you saying?" Collin and I were at odds, and I wasn't backing down.

"You know what, it's late, and this whole night has given me an epiphany."

"Epiphany!" I laughed.

"Yeah, that maybe this is your dream and not mine," he said solemnly.

"C, we just had a bad night. Let's shake it off, roll with the punches, keep it movin'!"

"I'm tired of the speeches, Blue. I keep fallin' right back into things with you. This time it's just not that easy for me to see that gleaming silver lining you always talk about. This time I gotta be realistic. I gotta be honest. I never saw all this. I saw getting into the best college and law school and being a lawyer.

"We failed, and I trusted you, regardless of how many times you kept jerking me around. I didn't go to that dinner tonight because of you. I bet my father's going to have a good time throwing this in my face. The fucked-up part is that I'm seeing that my dad might be right. Life isn't a party. I just gotta fall back and focus for a minute. Obviously I'm too caught up in your shit to handle my own business! This isn't *our* dream!" he said, throwing his hands in the air. "It's *your* dream."

"Oh, so it's all my fault? Hell no, C. There's business to handle. Shit happens. You don't give up!" I said, opening the door and getting out, leaving him hanging. "You call me when you figure out if you're still down!" I slammed the door and walked away. Collin screeched off. I had had enough of this entire night, and I didn't have the patience to pacify Collin. Blue Up was my baby, my brainchild. I wasn't about to let it slip away. With or without Collin.

I must've tried Jade at least six or seven more times. I typed one last message:

**I NEED U I WANNA COME TO THE HOSPITAL
WHERE R U? I LOVE U**

Jade typed back. My heart was racing.

IT'S MAMIE IT'S BEST U DON'T CALL BACK

It was six a.m. and I watched the sun come up. Still no sleep. All was lost with Jade. My partnership with Collin was in limbo. Maybe I ought to do like Collin and just do what my father wants. I decided to shoot a text to Whiteboy. The one thing about him is that whenever Collin and I had any kind of disagreement, he could shed some light, help us get things back on track.

YO WHAT HAPPENED 2NIGHT.

I pressed send.

The stakes were high, and I didn't pass the test. My back was up against the wall. It was all messed up now. I checked my Sidekick screen. No reply from Whiteboy. I threw my Sidekick across the room. It shattered into pieces.

WHAT COMES UP MUST COME . . .
HERE'S A LOOK AT THE SECOND BOOK IN THE COME UP SERIES:

CAN'T HOLD ME DOWN

In less than twenty-four hours I went from feeling like I was on top of the world to being at the bottom. I thought sleep would make it all go away. Unfortunately, I just kept having the same nightmare about the party at Club Heat last night. In it, everyone's dancing and having a good time, and then right before my eyes, tragedy strikes. The club suddenly goes up in flames, and all I hear are people shouting, *"Burn, Blue, burn!"* That's the end of the dream, and that's the end of Blue Up Productions.

I buried my head deeper into the pillow. I was sure all my peeps had been blowin' up my phone, especially Mamie and Tre, but screw it. Even if I wanted to talk to anybody right now, I couldn't since my phone was busted.

"Blue? Blue, it's Mom. You've got a phone call," she said, knocking loudly at my bedroom door.

"Just a minute!" I groggily replied, sitting up and wiping the sand out of my eyes. I checked the clock. It was seven a.m. on a Sunday. I couldn't imagine who the hell was calling me this early. I dragged myself out of bed and opened my bedroom door only to be greeted by my mother, fully dressed for church, with a pissed-off expression on her face.

"Your father and I are going to early service," she snapped. "Well, I don't know what exactly happened at that club party, but you've got some serious explaining to do. You were out until nearly four this morning. Based on the looks of things, is it safe to assume you're not going to church? Humph! I want this room spotless when I get back. Your father is furious!" She rolled her eyes and handed me the phone. "This isn't just going to go away. Your father wants to talk to you too," she snapped, slamming my bedroom door.

My life had just been washed down the drain, and now she was on my back. Whatever. I wasn't feeling moms, pops, or anything that either of them had to say.

"Hello?" I said groggily, putting the phone to my ear, plopping back down on my bed and leaning back.

"Yes, this is Holy Cross Hospital. I'm trying to reach a Blue Reynolds," an official-sounding voice said.

"Um, yeah, I mean yes, this is him speaking. Who is this?" I said, sitting up abruptly.

"We got two numbers to contact you, and I tried reaching you at two, four, zero . . ."

"Yeah, that line is down right now," I said, cutting her off, glancing across the room at the pieces of my broken cell staring back at me. "What's this about?" I was slightly agitated.

"Mr. Reynolds, I'm calling at the request of Tommy James," she said. I was wide awake now, but couldn't figure out who the hell Tommy James was.

"Who?"

"Sir, he says he's a friend of yours and he's a patient here at the hospital." Oh snap, she was talking about Whiteboy!

"Yeah, yeah, he is. What happened?" My heart raced.

"Well, he's pretty banged up, but he's resting well. He wrote down your name and two numbers as his emergency contact."

My head began to swell as she went on to explain how he had suffered some head trauma, but was fine. My brain was moving faster than my hand as I scribbled down the information the nurse was giving me. The first person I thought about was Collin. I needed to tell him, but my Sidekick was busted and I couldn't send him a text.

I figured I could call from the house phone, but since we weren't speaking, what would I say? I mean, I'd look like I was using Whiteboy being in the hospital as an excuse to call and apologize or something. On second thought, maybe it's best I got to the hospital, made an assessment of what was going on with Whiteboy, and *then* dealt with Collin.

I tried to keep myself calm on the short drive over to Holy Cross Hospital. All sorts of crazy thoughts were flying through my head about how Whiteboy was going to look. I wasn't sure what I'd be walking into. I prepared for the worst. My heart pounded faster and faster with each step down the bright hospital corridor.

The lone nurse sitting at the ICU station directed me to his room. I took a deep breath and slowly walked in. I don't think of myself as typically having a weak stomach, but seeing Whiteboy's face all wired up, and him hooked up to all the machines in that stark white room kind of freaked me out. I sat down slowly in the chair next to his bed. The nurse ran down Whiteboy's condition.

"Is he going to make it?" I said with a worried look.

"Definitely! No worries! It's just going to take some time. I know all these wires and things are a little scary, but that's just the IV giving him fluids." She pointed. "Because of his fractured jaw, he can't eat solid foods. That's how he gets fluids and nutrients. The other wires are to monitor his heart. He's got a couple broken ribs, too, and bruises and cuts mainly. It was pretty rough when he came in, but your friend is tough," she rattled off while checking his chart.

Whiteboy was definitely banged up, all black and blue like this. I felt awful looking at him with that wiring on his mouth. I bowed my head and said a silent prayer. When I looked up, Whiteboy was trying to open his eyes. He motioned for me to hand him the pen and paper that was sitting on the bedside table.

"Yo, Whiteboy, you've gotta rest, man," I said. He was adamant, pointing furiously to the pen. Whiteboy might have been in pain, but he was determined to write me a note. "Damn, yo, even in the hospital you're still a soldier." I chuckled, carefully handing him the pen and holding the pad of paper while he wrote. He managed to scribble "Collin" on the page.

How was I going to answer him? I shook my head, trying to give him some reassurance that Collin would be here. Except, the truth was, I was lying. I couldn't tell him that we weren't speaking. I couldn't tell him that the stupid fight *he* got into at the club was the cause of everything being messed up. Blue Up, me, Collin, Jade, Rico Tate, Young Tre, Ill Mama, it was all a wrap! My career as a club promoter was finished! Grand opening, grand closing, all in one night. I was starting to get mad all over again just thinking about it.

"He'll be here. Don't worry," I said, offering a reassuring smile. Whiteboy drifted off to sleep. After a while I must've drifted off too. I felt a light tap on my shoulder. I was being awakened by the nurse. She informed me that I'd have to leave the room so the doctor could examine him. I looked at the clock and realized I had been there for nearly an hour already. He was resting. It was a good time to take a break, maybe grab some coffee. When I stepped off the elevator on the main floor, I immediately thought about Jade. I knew she wasn't checking for me right now, but I figured since Holy Cross is the biggest hospital in Silver Spring, perhaps there was a chance she was here with her mom.

"Excuse me, I'm trying to find out if a Ms. Donna Taylor is a patient here," I said, leaning against the information desk. A few moments later the silver-haired woman looked up and smiled.

"Yes, she's on the second floor. You can check in at the east nurse's station."

Yes! There is a God! A bolt of energy shot through my body. I quickly dashed into the gift shop across the hall and scooped up a bouquet of flowers. A million thoughts ran through my head about Jade as I raced to the elevators. I pressed the up button. I just knew that when she saw me, she'd race into my arms and all would be forgiven. It was all just a dumb mix-up.

Even though I didn't know exactly what was wrong with her mom, I was sure Jade needed me right now. I *had* to be there for her. When the elevator doors opened I froze. I suddenly thought of Mamie's text after the party: IT'S BEST YOU DON'T CALL BACK. I stood there, stuck like a deer in headlights, trapped in quicksand.

"Son, are you getting on?" the lone elderly lady on the elevator asked. I shook my head. Maybe it was best to leave it be. The doors closed. I dumped the flowers in a nearby wastebasket. *Screw it!* I got my pride too.

I felt even more defeated about the whole Jade situation by the time I got back to the ICU floor where Whiteboy's room was. As I made my way down the hall, I could see him through the room's glass sliding door. I was suddenly smacked with guilt. *Collin should be here.* I owed it to him to tell him about Whiteboy being in the hospital. I had to put my anger aside.

Out of habit I reached for my cell to text him, and was quickly reminded it was out of commission. One of the nurses directed me to a phone. I was actually hoping Collin *wouldn't* answer since he probably wouldn't recognize the number. I was prepared to leave a message and keep it movin'.

After two rings Collin picked up.

"Hello?"

"Yo, it's me. Whiteboy's in ICU at Holy Cross," I said with short, direct words.

"I'm on my way."

There, I had done it, but only for the sake of Whiteboy, not because I was particularly interested in seeing Collin. I re-entered Whiteboy's room and plopped down in the chair next to his bed, closing my eyes and letting out a deep sigh. He was asleep. My stomach was beginning to knot up in anticipation of Collin's arrival. I think hospitals must have that effect on people. I put my face in my hands for several minutes, reflecting on the demise of the party again.

When I pulled them away, Collin was standing in the doorway. His chest was heaving as if he had sprinted all the way to the hospital. Collin slowly walked over to the bed. He pulled up a chair and sat down. Much like our phone conversation, we didn't even greet each other with hellos.

"What happened?" he asked through gritted teeth.

"They said there was some kind of accident. I'm thinkin' something went down with those cats he was beefin' with after the fight at the club," I snapped. "I don't know much else, except he drove himself to emergency."

"He's bad," he said, shaking his head.

"Real bad," I replied, putting my hand up to my mouth. "Broken ribs, busted jaw, bruises, cuts. They said he'll probably be wired up about four weeks." There was an uncomfortable silence. You could slice the tension in the air. It was all still too fresh. The only thing that kept flashing back to me were Collin's words from last night: *Maybe some things just aren't meant to be. . . .* When your best friend tells you something like that, it stings like salt on an open wound. You just don't shake it off that easily.

About the Author

Lyah Beth LeFlore, television producer and author, is one of today's most talented and respected creative forces. She's been featured in the *New York Times*, *Essence* magazine, *Ebony*, *Jet*, and *Entertainment Weekly*; also on CNN and BET. Television producer credits include: *New York Undercover* (FOX), *Midnight Mac* starring Bernie Mac (HBO), and *Grown Ups* (UPN). Her books include the coauthored *Cosmopolitan Girls*; the Essence bestseller *Last Night a DJ Saved My Life*; and the *New York Times* bestseller and *Essence* bestseller *I Got Your Back: A Father and Son Keep It Real About Love, Fatherhood, Family, and Friendship*—the nonfiction collaboration with Grammy Award father and son Eddie and Gerald Levert. *I Got Your Back* was a 2008 nominee/finalist for the *Essence* Literary Awards and the NAACP Image Awards. In 2008 Lyah also wrote the CD liner notes for The O'Jays' *The Essential O'Jays* and for multi-platinum artist Usher's *Here I Stand*. Lyah's third novel, *Wildflowers* (Broadway Books/Crown Publishing Group), arrives fall 2009. And now, with the hot new teen series The Come Up, she's expanding her fan base to include teen readers. Lyah, thirty-eight, is a native of St. Louis, Missouri, and holds a BA in Communications Media from Stephens College. In May 2005 she became the youngest member of the Stephens College Board of Trustees, and only the second African American to be appointed to the board in the college's history. She is also a member of the Alpha Kappa Alpha Sorority Incorporated. For more info go to lyahbethleflore.com.

About the Illustrator

DL Warfield is among the most consistent creative minds in visual branding, design, product and content development, youth culture, advertising, and marketing. His reputation has evolved from artistic mastermind to celebrated idea leader. He is a native of St. Louis, Missouri, and a graduate of Washington University's School of Fine Arts. He started his career as a product developer and creative consultant for the fashion retail corporation Edison Brothers Stores, Inc., creating logos and clothing designs for their super-successful Oaktree, Shifty's, and Factory brand divisions. Before long, Tommy Boy Records came calling, resulting in his acceptance of the title of head designer of the powerful record label's clothing line. Following an exciting tenure at Tommy Boy, DL became the resident art director at LaFace Records in Atlanta, Georgia. At LaFace, DL worked with some of today's hottest recording artists: Usher, TLC, OutKast, and Pink. He also received critical acclaim for designing the album artwork for OutKast's 1996 LP, *ATLiens*, as well as TLC's final album, *FanMail*. After LaFace shut its doors in 2000, DL launched his own company, GOLDFINGER c.s. Since its inception, clients include Nike, Sprite, Heineken, Anheuser-Busch, Geffen Records, Sony Latin Entertainment, DreamWorks Records, Sony Music, OutKast Inc., Universal Records, Nordstrom, RyanKenny Clothing Company, Arista Records, HBO, Virgin Records, Coca-Cola, Adidas, *Vibe*, GMC, and Song Airlines, to name a few. DL won the Bacardi Liquor "Cultural Architect" award in 2002; he was a finalist in the Hennessy Black Masters 2007 Art Competition; and in 2004 and 2005, DL was the winner of the Timberland Community Outreach Program, and commissioned to design a signature boot and mural in Atlanta for Timberland. As he continues to support various community awareness programs, his passion to diversify has only intensified, and the "creative crusader" is now intent on building cultural, social, and creative bridges.

TEENCENTRAL.NET®

totally **anonymous**. totally **cool.**

WWW.TEENCENTRAL.NET
LOG ON. WORK IT OUT.

SimonTeen

Simon & Schuster's **Simon Teen**
e-newsletter delivers current updates on
the hottest titles, exciting sweepstakes, and
exclusive content from your favorite authors.

Visit **TEEN.SimonandSchuster.com** to
sign up, post your thoughts, and find out what
every avid reader is talking about!